# What the critics are saying:

"Delivers...all the elements of a paranormal romantica that fans crave." ~ *Cindy Whitesel, Romantic Times Magazine*

"*BLOOD OATH* enthralls and captivates the reader." ~*Tracey West, The Road to Romance*

"I love [*Blood Oath*] as much as any of Christine Feehan's Dark series." ~*Oleta Blaylock, Just Erotic Romance Review Newsletter*

# Blood Oath

## BLOOD LINES BOOK I

# KIT TUNSTALL

ELLORA'S CAVE
ROMANTICA PUBLISHING

An Ellora's Cave Romantica Publication

www.ellorascave.com

Blood Oath

ISBN # 1419950320
ALL RIGHTS RESERVED.
Blood Oath Copyright© 2003 Kit Tunstall
Edited by: Ann Richardson
Cover art by: Christine Clavel

Electronic book Publication: May, 2003
Trade paperback Publication: August, 2005

# Warning:

The following material contains graphic sexual content meant for mature readers. *Blood Oath* has been rated E-*rotic* by a minimum of three independent reviewers.

Ellora's Cave Publishing offers three levels of Romantica™ reading entertainment: S (S-ensuous), E (E-rotic), and X (X-treme).

S-*ensuous* love scenes are explicit and leave nothing to the imagination.

E-*rotic* love scenes are explicit, leave nothing to the imagination, and are high in volume per the overall word count. In addition, some E-rated titles might contain fantasy material that some readers find objectionable, such as bondage, submission, same sex encounters, forced seductions, etc. E-rated titles are the most graphic titles we carry; it is common, for instance, for an author to use words such as "fucking", "cock", "pussy", etc., within their work of literature.

X-*treme* titles differ from E-rated titles only in plot premise and storyline execution. Unlike E-rated titles, stories designated with the letter X tend to contain controversial subject matter not for the faint of heart.

## Also by Kit Tunstall:

A Matter of Honor

Beloved Forever

Blood Lines: Blood Bond

Blood Lines: Blood Challenge

Blood Lines: Blood Price

By Invitation Only

Eye of Destiny

Heart of Midnight

Pawn

Phantasie

Playing His Game

The Twelve Quickies of Christmas

# Blood Oath

*Blood Lines*

# Prologue

*27 years ago…*

"What have you done?"

Demi jumped with fright at the angry sound of Valdemeer's voice carrying through the castle. He dropped the play sword on the floor of his bedroom with the *clunk* of wood against stone and ran in the direction of the shout. It sounded like it came from farther down the hallway of the children's wing.

He pumped his scrawny legs for speed as he rushed up the spiraled stone steps. Demi disdained the wooden handrail and conquered the steps with an ease born of youth. He turned down the passage and continued running. He heard Valdemeer's voice again, laced with anger, but the words weren't as distinct.

He nodded to the guard nearby as he veered through a set of tall wooden doors that had been propped open. He skidded to a halt at the sight before him.

Valdemeer held his six-year-old daughter by the lapels of her robe and was shaking her. "Answer me, Nikia," he demanded.

Demi's mouth dropped open with shock. In the four years he had lived at Castle Draganescu, he'd never heard the master raise his voice, nor witnessed any acts of violence.

Nikia's expression remained serene. The only indication of her emotions was the glittering anger in her brown eyes. "I disposed of the wench, Papa." She spoke with a calm belying her tender years.

Valdemeer growled with rage and thrust the girl away from him. Even in his anger, he was careful to make sure she wouldn't fall before he released her, Demi noticed.

He shook his head as he ran fingers through his thinning, brown-gray strands of hair. "Why would you send away your mother?"

Nikia's eyes darkened, and she spat out, "Stepmother."

Valdemeer sighed, and the flush of anger seemed to leave his cheeks slowly. His enraged expression changed to one of bewilderment. "She was kindness itself to you. Why?"

Nikia's lips compressed, and she looked pointedly at the wall. Her mouth curled when she saw Demi in the doorway. "Ask your spy, Papa. Perhaps he knows."

Valdemeer whirled around, his stance wary. His stiff posture relaxed when he saw Demi. He turned away from his daughter and walked toward Demi. Over his shoulder, he said, "This is not finished, Nikia. You are confined to your rooms."

Demi winced as Nikia shrieked her outrage and stamped her foot. Her wild auburn hair flew around her face in a thick cloud, giving her the appearance of wearing a halo of blood. As Valdemeer drew near, he turned his attention from the girl and bowed to his king. "What troubles you, sire?"

Valdemeer placed his hand on Demi's shoulder. "Walk with me, Nicodemus."

Demi fell in step beside the older man, pausing with him when the king stopped to speak with the guard. He waited silently while Valdemeer passed along instructions not to allow Nikia to leave her quarters.

Once more, they began walking. Demi wanted to ask again, but he didn't. He knew his king would speak when he was ready.

"You were Nikia's age when you came to the castle, weren't you?"

"Yes, sire."

Valdemeer shook his head. "You have proven yourself a faithful companion. You're like a son to me."

"Thank you, sire." Demi swallowed heavily, understanding what a compliment that was, in light of both of Valdemeer's sons dying—one in the womb, and the other when he was but a few days old.

Demi followed the king into his chambers. He stood silently while Valdemeer paced. "What's happened?" he asked again, after a long silence.

With a heavy sigh, Valdemeer dropped into a massive wooden chair. "Katrine has fled. She didn't say much in her note—only that she couldn't live in fear."

"Nikia," Demi whispered under his breath. God's truth, the young girl frightened him sometimes too, with her terrible rages and dark looks. "What did she do?" he asked in a louder tone.

Valdemeer shrugged. "She will not say, and Katrine didn't explain. I don't understand it, Nicodemus. Nikia was a toddler when I married Katrine. Yet, she refused to accept her from the beginning. When Julian was born, she became uncontrollable. I would have thought she was jealous, if she had ever enjoyed Katrine's company."

Demi cleared his throat. "I..." He trailed off, debating about the wisdom of saying anything.

The older man's brow quirked. "Yes, boy?"

"It probably means nothing, but I heard Nikia tell the cook's daughter, Sian, she would take the Blood Oath."

The king blinked, and then his eyelids dropped over his eyes. He fell into a long silence.

Demi stood by the door, wondering if he should say or do something. Finally, he licked his lips and said, "It isn't too late to stop Queen Katrine from leaving, is it? Even if she has arrived at the train station, you can stop her."

The silence continued for long seconds, broken only by the ticking of the ormolu clock on the mantle. Eventually, Valdemeer shook his head. "No, I can't stop her, son."

"But—"

"Perhaps it is for the best. Now that I suspect..." He stroked his full mustache. "They will be safer away from this place."

Demi frowned. "They, sire? Will you send Nikia away too?"

Valdemeer's brown eyes seemed to grow cloudier. "I can't. She is flesh of my flesh. What would I do with her? Where would I send her?"

Demi nodded his understanding, though he didn't fully grasp what his king meant. "Then who is 'they', sire?"

"My wife and child." Valdemeer's shoulder's drooped. "She is pregnant, Nicodemus. Katrine carries the one chosen for the Blood Oath. Your lifemate."

Demi's eyes widened. "You must bring her back immediately."

Valdemeer shook his head. "One day, she will return to Corsova, but not while she is a defenseless baby. For a time, she must remain far away from here." His head bowed forward. "May she and Katrine forgive me."

# Chapter One

Anca looked up as the bell on the door tinkled. Her eyes slid to the clock near the cash register, and she bit back a groan. Four minutes until closing. She plastered on a smile as her potential customer came into view.

The fake smile faded as she got a glimpse of him. She forgot how to breathe as the finest specimen of manhood she had ever seen strode to the front counter. He was well over six feet tall, with rippling muscles, a lean build, and silvery-blond hair that was a sharp contrast to his tanned skin and dark eyes. The perfect cut of his suit emphasized his magnificent physique, while contributing to his aura of power.

Or perhaps the suit had nothing to do with it. She swallowed heavily as he stopped in front of her. His chiseled lips didn't curve into a smile. Her mouth parted, and she couldn't seem to tear her gaze from him. Her nipples tightened against the lace of her bra, and she blushed, wondering if evidence of her arousal showed through the silk Nehru-style jacket she wore.

She glanced down and was relieved to see a barely discernable protrusion of her nipples against the pink fabric, silk-screened with roses. Her gaze returned to his when he cleared his throat. "Good evening," she said, pleased she didn't stumble over the words in her flustered state.

"Are you Anca Draganescu?" His voice was crisp and businesslike, but the accent underlying his words lent them a husky sensuality.

With that voice, he could make a discussion on weather turn her on. She almost giggled at the thought and strove to compose her features into a professional mask. "Yes. I'm the proprietor of *Dragan's Whimsy*."

He nodded. "You are a psychic, no?"

She shrugged. "I can't always control the gift—"

He interrupted before she could give her standard speech about no guarantees. "You will read me."

Her eyes widened at his imperious command. "The store will be closing soon, sir. I'd be happy to schedule an appointment for you tomorrow. I had a cancellation just this afternoon."

He shook his head. "Impossible, Miss Draganescu. Now, please."

She took a deep breath, struggling to maintain control of her temper. Even though he looked as though he'd stepped from a *GQ* ad, that didn't give him the right to be rude. "That is impossible. Tomorrow."

"I will be on my way home by tomorrow. My flight leaves at midnight." He glanced at his watch as he pushed back the cuff of his suit and light-blue shirt. "I took the liberty of flipping your closed sign and locking the door."

Anca's mouth fell open. "That's unacceptable. How dare you?"

"I will pay any amount." His eyes softened. "You must do this."

She frowned, disconcerted when the anger forming banked at his gentler expression and lowered tone. "Why is it so important?"

He shrugged. "I must appease my curiosity."

She sighed. "Fine, but I'll expect double the standard fee." Anca turned the key to lock the register and slipped the ring in the pocket of her silk slacks. "Please make yourself comfortable while I brew tea."

He walked to the beige suede sofa and chairs in the corner of the store without responding. Anca watched him take a seat before she left her post behind the counter and went to the tea cozy in the opposite corner. The water in the pot was still hot, and she selected her special blend of jasmine, chamomile, and lemon verbena tea, used to enhance consciousness.

She added two scoops of the leaves to a small ceramic pot. Anca measured water from the metal pot on the warmer and added it to the teapot decorated with roses and ribbons. While it steeped, she added matching teacups and saucers to a silver tray. When they were arranged aesthetically, she put the small steeping pot on the tray and carried it over to her customer.

He had chosen the sofa, and he was leaning back against the cushions. There was an aura of grace about his movements as he shifted to sit up straight. "What's the tea for?" He eyed the pot as though it contained something less innocuous than tea.

Anca smiled at him as she lifted a cup and saucer to pour the brew. "It aids in relaxation. The more open you are, the more I'll be able to pick up."

He lifted a brow as he took the cup she had filled.

She watched with amusement as he sniffed the contents before sipping it. He frowned, but didn't thrust it away. She poured a cup for herself and took the chair closest to him. "May I ask why you want a reading, sir? What do you hope to learn today?"

Anca sipped her tea, waiting to hear the standard questions: *When will I be promoted? Will I get married? Should we have children? Are my wife and I drifting apart?* Her eyes sought out his left hand and saw the ring finger lacked a gold band, but that didn't mean anything.

His gaze was forthright when he met hers. "I want to see if you're who I think you are."

She swallowed without thought, not expecting such an answer, and unable to form a coherent reply. The hot tea burned her tongue, and she gasped. Who did he think she was?

"Are you all right, Miss Draganescu?"

Anca waved her hand before setting the cup on the tray. "I'm fine. Shall we begin, Mr....?" The sooner they finished, the sooner she could get him out of her shop. Once upstairs in her apartment, her unease would fade away, she assured herself.

"Demi Golina." He didn't offer his hand to shake.

"May I see your hand, Mr. Golina?"

His eyes narrowed. "Are you a palm reader, Miss Draganescu?" His tone bordered on scathing.

She shook her head. "No. I simply find touch the easiest way to read someone."

He extended his hand.

Anca folded it between hers, careful not to rake his flesh with her long nails. She cried out as soon as they touched. Visions raced through her mind in a dizzying array of colors and sound, with little form. She had never experienced anything like it before.

She tried to jerk away, but only succeeded in freeing one hand. He tightened his grip on the other. She cried out again, begging him with a jumble of incoherent sounds to release her.

"Tell me what you see, Anca," he purred. He looked intense, but there wasn't a trace of cruelty on his face. He didn't seem to receive any pleasure from prolonging the contact or causing her fear.

"A-a ch-chalice," she stuttered. "Gold, antique, with a ruby in its handle..." She shook her head as the cup left her mind, replaced by a vision that had color sweeping up her neck.

Mr. Golina had her bent backwards over a table, and she moaned as he sucked on her nipple. From the waist up, they were both nude. Pressed together, they struggled to get even closer. Anca heard a moan escape her lips, and it held the same passion as in her vision.

"What is it?"

She shook her head, unable to describe the scene. When she met his eyes, she saw a half-smile curved his lips, and his eyes had darkened. Was he experiencing the same vision? She had never shared one with another person before. She had only relayed what she saw in the past.

She broke eye contact and closed her eyes. Anca shook her head, struggling to dispel the vision. She counted slowly to ten, which was usually enough to break her concentration if a vision became too vivid. This time, it only increased in clarity. As he continued to suckle at her breast, his hand slid down her stomach, into the waistband of her pants, and over her panties.

Anca jerked in the chair as he stroked her pussy in the vision. She grew wet in real life, and she was already dripping with need in the vision. Her pussy spasmed with yearning as his fingers explored her.

The experience was disconcerting enough to cause her eyes to fly open. Anca tore her hand from his. "No more, please. I don't see anything at all."

He chuckled. "Didn't your mother raise you not to fib, Anca?"

"You must go now, Mr. Golina. No charge for the reading." Anca bounded from the seat and began stacking the cups haphazardly on the tray. She stiffened when he touched her arm, but the visions didn't return. She breathed a small sigh of relief.

"I can't just yet."

"Why not?" A flash of the vision returned to her, along with a quiver of fear. Did this man plan to rape her? Anca frowned, remembering how aroused she was in the vision. It didn't fit.

"My purpose in coming here wasn't for a reading. I was sent to find you, Anca."

Her eyes widened. "By who?"

He took a deep breath. "Your father."

Anca dropped the tray she had just lifted, and it fell with a small clatter onto the wooden table. "That's a lie. My father is dead."

Mr. Golina shook his head. "No. He lives, and he's anxious to meet you. He's waited so long."

Her mouth fell open, and she struggled to speak. "That's another lie. I've been here in New York the past twenty-six years. He could have found me."

He ran a hand through his short, blond hair. "He's dying, Anca. He needs to see you now."

She shook her head. "He's dead. My mother told me he died before I was born."

"Katrine was trying to protect you."

Suspicion clouded her eyes. "My mother's name is Kathryn, and you've just blown your entire scam. Get out of here before I call the police."

He sighed heavily. "It is no confidence game that brings me here, I assure you. I'm acting as the emissary of your father, whose dying wish is to meet his daughter. Will you deny him?"

She tilted her chin. "I don't believe you."

"You wear a ruby pendant around your neck," he said softly. "You never take it off."

Anca frowned at his knowledge, but she bluffed her way through. "That's no big secret. Last year, one of my clients tried to buy it from me. When I wouldn't sell it, she hired someone to steal it. It was in the papers."

His brow furrowed, and he muttered something that sounded like a name under his breath. "Yes, I'm sure it was her," he said more loudly. He looked thoughtful, but then he blinked, and his expression returned to one of earnestness as he dismissed the topic of the attempted theft. "At different times of the year, the pendant seems to glow with an internal light. It warms to the touch."

"I..." Anca broke off, unable to reply. She hadn't told anyone about that, fearing they would think she had gone nuts.

"You've always had the pendant."

She nodded, not able to remember a time when she didn't wear it.

"Your mother took it with her when she fled the castle and Corsova. Katrine knew what it represented, and she knew it was your birthright."

"What are you talking about? My mother is an immigrant from the Ukraine."

Mr. Golina shook his head emphatically. "No, she was born in the Corsovan village of Rij, at the starting point of the Bulgain Mountains. Romania and Moldova border our country, as does the Ukraine, but she never visited that country, to my knowledge. Katrine spent her whole life in her village, until she married your father when she was seventeen. She ran away after they had been married four years. That was the first time she left the borders of Corsova."

Anca clapped her hands over her ears. "That isn't true. I know my mother."

He grasped her wrists and pried away her arms. "She left your father, who had much affection for her. He worries about her even to this day. She loved him deeply, but she took you from him, to protect you."

"What kind of monster is my father then, that I would have to be protected?" she asked stridently.

"Valdemeer is a good man. She fled from…others who would do his heir harm."

Anca wilted and slumped forward. He still held her wrists, and she was inches from touching him. "I don't want to know any of this."

His expression didn't hold a shred of pity. "You must know the truth. You have to come back with me to meet your father, before it's too late. Time grows short, Anca. We have less than a month." He released her wrists.

Anca sank into the chair she had vacated. Automatically, her hand went to the pendant under her shirt. She lifted it by the chain, until the stone rested against her hand. It was warm to the touch, and it glowed softly. Specks of gold illuminated the stone, and she frowned. It had never done that before.

Mr. Golina knelt beside her chair. "Will you come? I have us booked on a midnight flight."

Anca bit her lip, torn between the chance to meet a man she had thought was dead and the opportunity to hurt him as he had hurt her, by rejecting his dying wish. She sighed, knowing there would be little satisfaction in denying him. Her pride would be cold comfort after his death, when it was too late to meet him if she changed her mind.

She nodded slowly. "I'll come."

A small smile lifted his lips. "Excellent, Anca."

She frowned at him. "What's he like, Mr. Golina?"

He shrugged. "Valdemeer is a difficult man to describe. You will see for yourself soon enough." He rose to a standing position and offered her a hand.

Anca took it reluctantly, preparing herself for an onslaught of visions. Nothing happened. She stood up, but when she tried to loosen his hold, he grasped her hand more firmly. She stared up at him with confusion.

"We will be good friends, Anca. I would very much like it if you called me Demi."

She nodded, grateful she didn't blurt out what she was thinking. If the revelation were true, they would be more than friends. A lot more, indeed.

# Chapter Two

Demi waited without speaking as Anca went through the nightly procedures to close the store. Once she had washed the tea items and put the deposit in a night drop bag, she walked to the front of the store to double check the lock he'd said he clicked. It was secure, and when she turned around, she found him standing too close for comfort. Her heart rate sped up.

"You didn't believe me?" The question might have been irritating, if his attitude hadn't indicated he didn't care if she believed him.

Anca shrugged. "This is my livelihood, Mr.—Demi. It's not a matter of trust."

He inclined his head. "I understand."

"My mother and I live above the store." She gestured he should follow her as she made her way into the backroom. They passed through the mini-kitchen/lounge with the foldout sofa and walked to the staircase. "I'll need to speak with her."

She could feel him following her up the stairs, just a hair's breadth away. Anca bit her lip, concentrating on the worn carpet and stepping onto each stair. His cologne smelled of the outdoors, and she had the impulse to turn around and bury her nose in the hollow of his throat.

Anca blinked the thought away as they stepped onto the second-floor landing. He brushed against her back, and she caught her breath. A surge of emotion followed the light contact, and she cleared her throat to regain her focus.

She turned to face him before they entered the living room cordoned off by a thick curtain. "My mother is fragile. I would appreciate it if you don't upset her."

Demi's brow arched. "Won't your news upset her?"

Anca shook her head. "I won't tell her where I'm going."

He frowned. "She is your mother. Surely, she should know."

She sighed. "Please, trust me. She had a bypass earlier this year and doesn't need the stress."

He hesitated before nodding once. She took it for a yes, slid open the curtain, and entered the confines of the small living room.

The TV was on, but the lights were off. Kathryn was curled on the couch, clutching a tissue to her breast as tears rolled down her cheeks.

Anca glanced at the TV and saw a black-and-white movie playing. Her mother was sentimental about such things. She felt for the light switch and flipped it. Dim light from the forty-watt bulb illuminated the room. "Mother, we have a visitor."

Kathryn's head whipped up, and she crushed the tissue in a tighter hold. Her thin face was almost as pale as the white Kleenex, except for the purple bags under her eyes. She frowned at Demi. "Who's he?"

Anca realized her mother and Demi had the same accent, though Kathryn's had softened during the time she had lived in America. "This is Mr. Golina."

He bowed to her. "Madam."

Kathryn wore a frown, and her brow was furrowed. "Golina," she repeated softly.

"I'll be going on a short business trip, Mother."

Kathryn's eyes widened, and she shifted her gaze from Demi to Anca. "What? Why?"

"Mr. Golina knows of a rare herb perfect for tea, and it grows only in his country. He's offered to show me where I can find it." Anca felt the story flow from her tongue easily. It almost felt like they hadn't been her words. She tensed, waiting to see if her mother would question her excuse.

Her mother's frown deepened, but she didn't dispute the reason for the trip. "How long will you be gone?"

"Several weeks." Demi's quiet tone brooked no argument.

Anca's eyes widened, and she shot him a look. "I can't possibly stay that long, Mr. Golina."

"Anything less would be unacceptable," he said softly.

"I have a business to run, a life here in New York. I can't stay for more than a few days."

He looked annoyed, and his mouth opened. His eyes darted to Kathryn before moving back to Anca, and he closed his mouth with a click. He nodded. "If that's all the time you can spare, it will be appreciated."

She sighed at the averted argument, though she couldn't help wondering if he would resurrect it when they were out of her mother's presence. "I'll be back within a week, Mother."

"I can run the shop for you."

Anca swallowed down an automatic no and forced herself to nod, knowing her mother wouldn't appreciate being coddled. "I would be grateful if you booked appointments and handled the customers. There are two-dozen orders of specialty teas waiting to mail out to customers. You'll find the boxes and invoices in my office. Please call my clients booked for readings this week and tell them I'll reschedule when I return. Offer them a twenty-five-percent discount."

Kathryn nodded, and once again, her gaze moved to Demi. "Your name is familiar to me, Mr. Golina."

"Hmm," he said, without meeting her eyes.

"I'll go pack," Anca told Demi.

Her mother frowned. "You're leaving tonight?"

She nodded. "The flight is at midnight."

"Where are you going?" Kathryn sounded strained.

"Romania," Demi said. "The flight lands in Constanta."

Anca nodded again. "If you'll excuse me?" She left the living room before either could protest or add something more. She hoped Demi would keep his silence about who he was and where they were going.

\* \* \* \* \*

Katrine didn't speak or issue an invitation to sit. Demi sat down on a lumpy chair after standing for a moment in her presence. She stared at him with wide brown eyes, as she nibbled on her lower lip.

Valdemeer had asked him to note Katrine's appearance and living conditions. He would be expecting a full report on his wife, and Demi knew he wouldn't be pleased to hear she had been sick, or they lived at a level well below what should have been theirs by right.

"I know who you are," she said with sad resignation, though a hint of anger darkened her eyes. Katrine's face drew into a scowl. "Little Nicodemus, all grown up. You've come to take my daughter." She made it a statement, not a question.

He weighed his promise to Anca not to upset her mother against outright lying. He sighed. "Yes, m'lady."

She laughed, and it was a hard sound. "I am no lady here."

"You will always be my queen."

She swallowed, and the edge of resentment seemed to leave her face and voice. "Did Valdemeer remarry?"

He shook his head.

Katrine closed her eyes and grasped a strand of rosary beads. She seemed to be praying. When she opened them and met his gaze, she shook the strand. "I converted when we arrived in New York. A priest was kind to me. He helped me find work and get settled."

"His Majesty would have seen to your comforts."

She shrugged. "What right did I have to take anything from him?" Her voice dropped. "Haven't I taken enough, dear boy?"

He left her question unanswered, except to say, "Perhaps your reasons were compelling, madam."

She sighed heavily. "Why are you here?"

"His Majesty wishes to meet Anca." He hesitated over saying anything more. Finally, he added. "He's ready to die."

"Mary, Mother of God," she whispered as she crossed herself. "It's time, isn't it?"

He nodded, wondering if she would attempt to stop it.

Katrine sat up slowly and leaned forward. She dropped the tissue on the table before grasping one of his hands in hers. "You will guard her, won't you?"

He nodded.

"Valdemeer chose you as her Protector during your journey?"

Demi nodded again. "But I'm more than that."

Her eyes widened. "You're her lifemate, aren't you?"

"Yes, m'lady, if she will have me."

Tears slipped from the corner of Katrine's eyes. "I won't see him again. I always thought someday…"

"Come with us," he said impulsively. "You would be a comfort to Valdemeer."

Katrine shook her head. "I can't be there for it. I know what happens when she takes the Blood Oath."

Demi squeezed her hand. "He'll understand."

"Tell him…" she trailed off.

"I will relay any message you wish, m'lady."

She released his hand to brush the tears from her cheeks. "Tell him I am sorry, and I love him. I know I wasn't his destined lifemate, but I wanted to make him happy." She sniffed. When she regained her composure, she said, "He knows the rest, I pray."

"I'm sure he does." Demi hesitated, feeling the need to comfort the woman. "I think Valdemeer loved you as much he could…he held great affection for you, m'lady."

He winced at how insensitive that sounded. "I mean, with Madra—"

"Shh, dear boy, I know what you mean." A faint smile crossed Katrine's lips. "He could never love me as much as he loved her, but he loved me well enough. If only…" She blinked, and her eyes cleared. "I am entrusting my daughter to you. I invoke you to uphold your vow to protect her."

"With my life," he said solemnly.

Her lips trembled, and she took a moment to speak. "More than that, I implore you to treat her well and love her."

"With all my heart." Demi's eyes didn't shift from her gaze, and he allowed a hint of his emotions to show.

Katrine nodded, apparently satisfied.

# Chapter Three

Despite the luxurious seating in first class, Anca's legs hurt from being on the plane for nearly two days. As soon as they were inside the terminal at Kogalniceanu Airport in Constanta, she set down her carryon and stretched. The muscles in her back loosened gradually, and her legs stopped cramping.

As she twisted her neck, Anca looked in Demi's direction and discovered his gaze rested on her breasts. She froze, waiting for a reaction. He didn't seem to realize she had caught him yet, and his eyes remained focused on her nipples, poking through her white shirt. The thin cotton clearly revealed the outline of her lacy bra, and his eyes didn't deviate from the sight.

Experimentally, she thrust forward her chest, under the guise of stretching her back again. His eyes widened, and he stiffened. Abruptly, his gaze moved from her chest to her face. His expression was inscrutable.

Anca hastily broke eye contact and bent down to lift her case, wondering at her impulse to tempt him. Why was a reaction from him so important? She sighed quietly as she followed him through the busy terminal to the luggage carousel. Perhaps she wanted to ensure the attraction she felt for him wasn't one-sided.

After claiming her luggage, they negotiated their way through the terminal. Anca was surprised at the variety of people mingling. There were men and women dressed professionally walking side-by-side with others who looked as though they could have stepped from a book on the history of fashion.

As soon as they stepped through the doors and into the sunlight, Anca blinked. The brightness of the afternoon light hurt her eyes, but it was a welcome respite from the dim interiors of the planes and lounges they had passed through in the past day-and-a-half. When her eyes adjusted, she glanced at Demi.

He was blinking rapidly, and he had averted his face down toward the sidewalk. He slipped sunglasses from the pocket of his suit jacket. Once they were in place, he lifted his head again. "My eyes are sensitive."

"I see."

"Are you hungry?"

Anca nodded.

Demi glanced at his watch. "We'll be at Gara Constanta soon enough."

"What's Gara Constanta?"

Before answering, Demi lifted his arm to catch the attention of a driver at the curb. "The train station."

She frowned. "How far away is Corsova?"

"The border is about 160 kilometers away. It's another 40 to the capitol, where we'll get off the train. Beyond that, Castle Draganescu is another 30 kilometers."

Anca's brow furrowed as she tried to remember metric conversions. "Um, that's about 175 miles, isn't it?"

"More like 140," he said as they walked toward the cab. The driver had exited his car and opened the trunk for them as they neared. Demi placed his small bag in first, then her two suitcases he had insisted on carrying.

Anca put her carryon in with the rest of the bags and walked around to the back of the cab. She was conscious of Demi's proximity as she opened the door and slipped inside. Within seconds, he sat next to her, with his thigh pressed against hers. Was it because the seat of the Mini was small, or did he enjoy touching her?

She wet her lips. "Why didn't we just fly into...what is the capitol of Corsova?"

"Bulgainia," he said, before sliding forward to give the driver instructions to take them to the train station. When he leaned back against the seat, he turned his face to her. "There is no airport in Corsova."

Her eyes widened. "How do you manage without an airport?"

Demi shrugged. "Imports arrive by train in the capitol, or they are shipped to the harbor at Vachow. We have no need for an airport."

She frowned. "What about the convenience? Aren't your citizens bothered by having to travel more than two hundred miles, er, kilometers if they want to take a trip?"

Demi shrugged, but didn't reply.

Anca sighed and turned to look out the window. Grayish stone buildings dominated the architecture, but encroaching Western influence was making itself known. The streets weren't the narrow cobblestones she might have imagined. There was little difference from the streets she was used to, except that Constanta wasn't nearly as populated as New York.

She turned back to him. "Is Bulgainia as large?"

Demi shook his head. "Constanta has about 350,000 citizens. Bulgainia has ten thousand or so."

"Is that your largest city?"

He nodded. "The population is spread out among the villages and towns of our country. There are less than one million Corsovans."

Anca shook her head in wonder. She had imagined Corsova was a small country, but she couldn't fathom it having so small a populace. She lived in a city with more than eight million. How would she adjust?

Fortunately, she didn't have to adjust, she reminded herself. Within a week, this visit would be a memory, and she would be home. She felt an unexpected surge of nostalgia for the crowded streets and smoggy air of New York as the taxi wove through the traffic.

She blinked back silly tears as a car cut in front of their cab. The driver waited patiently. She wished he would scream obscenities at the offender, so it would seem more like home.

"You're quiet."

Anca turned her head to look at him. "I'm a little homesick. Constanta is a lot more like New York than I would have imagined, but it isn't home." He touched her hand, causing a current of awareness to shoot up her arm. Her lips parted, and she expelled a harsh breath.

He didn't offer platitudes. Instead, he said, "We're approaching the train station. Soon, you will see your father's home."

She tried to make her smile confident, but it felt shaky at the edges.

The driver stopped in front of Gara Constanta, angling into a narrow parking space left by a departing cab. Demi slid out first, offering his hand to assist her.

Anca took it as she scooted across the seat, though she didn't need his help. A shiver worked its way up her spine as his warm hand closed around hers. A dart of disappointment flashed through her when she exited the car and he dropped her hand.

The driver got out of the Mini to open the small trunk for them. He bobbed his head when Demi handed him a wad of bills. With a cheery farewell, he returned to the cab. Within seconds, three men were pushing their way past Anca and Demi to get into the car.

She stepped back from the men, holding firmly to her carryon. All around her, Anca heard a babble of voices speaking a language she didn't understand. The train station was modern, but it still seemed alien to her. Having Demi beside her was strangely reassuring, though he was as alien as anything else surrounding her.

He tucked her bags under his arms and held his bag. "We'll get our tickets and secure our luggage on the train. Once we're settled, we'll pick up something to eat in the dining car."

"Okay." Her stomach grumbled at the mention of food, and she followed him with renewed vigor. Nerves at the upcoming meeting with her father still caused her stomach to churn with nausea, but hunger was making its presence felt.

When they stepped into the train station, Anca's eyes scanned the boards with the schedules. Each schedule was in three languages, but she didn't know any of them.

Demi walked to the ticket counter without a pause in his step. He set down the suitcases and peeled off a few bills from the bundle he withdrew from his pocket. He asked for two tickets in a language she didn't recognize. The short, balding clerk quickly processed their request and slid two tickets across the counter, along with a key ring.

As he returned the money, key ring, and tickets to his pocket, Anca's eyes caught the money clip around the wad of bills. It was gold, etched with intricate swirls. A tear-shaped ruby gleamed in the center of the clip, cupped by two hands etched from gold. She reached out to touch it. "It's beautiful."

He slipped the clip in his pocket. "It is the symbol of our country. It represents our Protector shielding the life source of our people."

A frisson of fear worked its way down her spine, though she had no reason to be afraid of his words. "What is the life source?" Life source sounded so…ominous.

Demi hesitated. Finally, he shrugged. "I don't remember what the ruby represents. The symbol is as old as Corsova itself."

She studied him more closely. His eyes slid from hers, and she knew he was lying. Why? "How old is that?"

He shrugged. "Some say as old as time."

Anca turned when someone spoke sharply behind them. The man seemed irritated with them, and she realized they were blocking the line.

After lifting their bags, Demi voiced a soft apology to the impatient customer, and they moved deeper into the station.

She stayed near him, feeling overwhelmed by the odd similarities and striking differences between Gara Constanta and Grand Central Station. "When does our train leave?"

"Twenty minutes." He walked without hesitation through the station, leading her to the right platform.

Anca followed him onto the train, and they moved through four passenger cars before entering a car with doors on each side of the corridor, but no open seating. Her stomach clenched as he began reading the numbers. Had he booked them into a private compartment?

They moved through two more cars before he stopped before a door marked 15. "This is our compartment."

She cleared her throat. "Ours?"

He turned to her, quirking his brow. "Is there a problem?"

She licked her lips nervously. Anca was unable to say she didn't want to be confined to close quarters with him. "It seems like an extravagance, is all. We'll only be on the train for..." She trailed off, not able to finish her statement without knowing how long the journey was.

"You can spend the next two hours resting, Anca. It's nicer to travel in a quiet compartment than amid the masses." He put down the case in his left arm and fished the key from his pocket. He opened the door and stepped back, indicating she should precede him.

She swallowed the lump in her throat and stepped into the private compartment. Anca flipped on the light and grimaced. It was as small as she had feared. A small table and two chairs, positioned near the sole window, were bolted to the floor. A loveseat was near the table, and there was a low shelf she assumed was supposed to pass for a bunk built into the wall below an overhead luggage rack. The bunk was barely big enough for one.

She moved aside so Demi could enter. He brushed against her side with his stomach, and her flesh suddenly seemed hypersensitive. She imagined she could feel the warmth emanating from his skin through her shirt. "It's cozy," she said with forced cheerfulness.

He didn't bother to respond as he stacked their luggage on the rack. His expression was inscrutable when he turned back to face her. "Would you like to accompany me for a drink?"

She shook her head. "I'm tired." She ignored the twinges of hunger in her stomach and pasted on a smile. "I think I'll lie down for a while."

He walked to the door.

Anca frowned when she realized he wasn't going to say anything. For some reason, that irked her. It must be too much effort to try to convince her, or ask if she would rather eat than drink. After all, he'd been the one to suggest they eat on the train, when they could have stopped at that McDonald's they passed on the way. She glared at his departing back, but jumped with surprise when he whirled around.

She attempted to smooth her expression into one more innocent as he stood there staring at her, without speaking. She cleared her throat to break the thick silence. "Yes?"

"I have the key, so I will let myself in."

She nodded.

"Don't let in anyone else. I'll deal with the ticket agent so he doesn't disturb you."

Her eyebrows felt as if they rose of their own accord. "Um, okay." Who else would come into their car?

He nodded briskly and turned away to open the door. He stepped through and closed it behind himself. The sound of the key turning in the lock followed his departure.

Anca paced the confines of the private compartment, frowning at his strange edict. She went over his words in her mind several times, but couldn't find any reason for his warning.

Her legs seemed to go boneless, and she collapsed onto the narrow bunk. What if the people her mother had protected her from were still after her? Was she putting herself in danger by going into Corsova? Did someone still think she was a threat?

If she hadn't been so afraid, the idea would have been laughable. She could assure anyone who might be worried that she wanted no part of her father's wealth or status. And, surely, he must have both, if someone had tried to harm his heir.

The people she knew had no need to protect their heirs from scheming machinations and attempted assassinations. Betsy at the beauty shop couldn't care less who took over her lease when she retired, and no one would challenge Jimmy Phoung for control of his father's deli when Phoung-Li passed on.

Anca shook her head, unable to imagine herself the heir to anything. In truth, she didn't want any inheritance from her father. She only wanted to meet him while she still had the chance, and then return to her real life in New York.

Staying in Corsova to follow in his footsteps—or whatever would be required from her—was the last thing she would ever want to do. She would make her father and everyone else realize that during her visit. There wouldn't be any danger once that realization sank in.

She felt slightly more in control once she had a plan in mind. If everyone in Corsova were as commanding as

Demi, Anca knew she would have to be firm, but she could do that. After all, she was a businessperson and knew how to stick to a plan until she reached a goal.

In this case, her goal was to leave Corsova without losing her life or her heart. She sensed Demi was more dangerous to the latter than any power-hungry schemers could be to the former.

A wave of tiredness swept over Anca, and she yawned. The narrow bunk seemed more appealing than it had a few minutes ago, and she stretched out on it. It wasn't as uncomfortable as it looked. The swaying motion of the train, coupled with the rhythmic sound of the wheels on the track, soon lulled her to sleep.

*The night sky was a black canvas, with thousands of stars twinkling overhead. She had never seen anything like it in New York. She could hear the wind blowing softly through the trees. The lone cry of a wolf rose with haunting intensity, before others soon joined in, and their cries echoed down the mountainside. The pack was close, but she felt no fear.*

*The tumescent moon was nearly full, and it had a strange pinkish cast. Each time her eyes sought it, her heartbeat accelerated. She turned her head at the touch of lips again+t her wrist.*

*"Soon, it will be time," Demi said, and his lips tickled her skin. "In two nights, the moon will be blood-red."*

*"Yes." She knew exactly what he was speaking of, but she couldn't recall it when she tried to. Her brow furrowed, and she started to ask what they were talking about, but her eyes widened when Demi's teeth penetrated the skin at her wrist, finding the vein unerringly.*

*She gasped as the initial pain faded to an intense pleasure. Anca held her breath, and her eyes closed of their own volition. She was propped on her elbow, lying in a field in the middle of the night, but it didn't seem strange to her. She opened her eyes to slits and watched the play of emotions on Demi's face. As his throat worked convulsively, swallowing her blood, she laid back on the soft bed of rose bay.*

*He retracted his fangs and released her wrist as he moved up her body. Her blood smeared his lips, and Anca lifted her head to hasten the meeting of their mouths. Rather than kiss him, she traced her tongue across his lips, licking away the traces of her blood. The flavor was pungent and coppery, but with an underlying sweetness that made her yearn for more.*

*Demi had been sprawled beside her, but now he broke away and rolled over to straddle her. He braced his hands on the ground, bracketing her head, and he leaned forward to kiss her. His cock pressed into the softness of her stomach, and her pussy flooded with desire.*

*Anca tilted her head, offering her neck for his possession, but he ignored the temptation. Instead, his lips parted hers gently, and his tongue ventured inside to explore her moist depths. She groaned low in her throat as his tongue slid across hers. She tried to trap it between her tongue and cheek, and he chuckled into her mouth.*

*His tongue retreated, and he eased his weight down on her more fully. As Demi's face burrowed into the bend of her neck, one of his hands squeezed her breast. He rubbed a nipple between his fingers, causing the sensitive nub to harden at his expert touch.*

*His other hand traveled down her side, exploring her ribs, pausing to span her waist, before moving past her hip, and sliding along her thigh.*

*Anca stiffened as he sought out her pussy. He was going too slowly. She longed to feel his cock inside her, and anticipation had her gyrating her hips impatiently.*

*He chuckled again as he stroked her swollen pussy lips, wet with her own dew, but he didn't venture between them.*

*She grunted and arched her hips, demanding without words that he fulfill his unspoken promise.*

*Demi's breath was hot against her neck when he said, "So impatient."*

*She tangled her hands in his hair, urging his mouth closer to her neck as she arched her hips. "Please," she whispered.*

*"I live to serve you," he said with a trace of gentle mockery. Seconds later, his fangs penetrated the vein at her neck at the same time his fingers slid inside her pussy and sought out her twitching clit. He found her wet and ready, and she gave voice to her passion…*

*"Anca!"*

Her eyes snapped open, and she expelled a harsh breath. Demi's face was inches from her own, and she first thought she was still in the dream. Her pussy was wet and aching, and her nipples were hard. It was only when she realized his expression was concerned, rather than passionate, that Anca knew she wasn't dreaming. "What?" she managed to ask in a dry voice.

"You were dreaming. I heard you groan, and then you cried out." Demi removed his hands from her shoulders, where he had apparently been shaking her to get her to awaken. "Were you having a nightmare?"

Anca shook her head and let that be her answer. She remembered every aspect of the dream as clearly as if she had really experienced it. She wasn't telling Demi any of the details.

"I've brought you food—"

As he spoke, the train went around a sharp bend, and he fell forward. He landed across her body, and the full weight of his arousal pressed against her thigh.

Anca's eyes widened when she felt his cock against her. Hesitantly, she met his eyes and saw they had darkened. Flecks of silver seemed to glow around his pupils. The vein in his temple throbbed visibly, in time with the throbbing of his cock. He was clearly aroused. Had he seen her dream?

She tried to shove away that disconcerting thought. Anca cleared her throat. "You said something about food?"

A dull red seeped into his cheeks, and he scrambled off her. "Er, yes. I knew you were hungry." He glanced at his watch, and the action held a hint of stiffness, as though he was desperate to avoid her eyes. "You've been asleep for more than an hour. You should have enough time to eat and freshen up before we arrive in Bulgainia."

Anca was determined to ignore her state of arousal, so she struggled to convince herself that her nipples weren't still hard and aching. He couldn't possibly see them through the cotton of her shirt. Even if he could, well…she couldn't do anything about it.

She put on her most professional face, the one reserved for dealing with suppliers and testy customers, and swung her legs off the bunk. She saw a tray on the table by the window and stood up.

Anca swayed as the train rocked under her. When Demi reached out a hand to steady her, she smiled at him. "Thank you. I'm not accustomed to train travel." Despite being a native New Yorker, she had seldom used Grand

Central Station for transportation, other than to board the subways.

His hand was slow to drop away. "Of course."

Anca allowed her feet to fall into the rhythm of the train, and it wasn't as erratic as she had expected. She made her way to the table and dropped into a chair. She looked up to see Demi standing uncertainly in the center of the car. "Will you join me?"

He nodded and came to sit with her, after pausing to turn on the lamp bolted to the wall. The sun was hanging low in the sky, and shadows filled the compartment, until the dim illumination chased them away.

Anca stared at the food on the plate. There was a covered plate and bowl, and a carafe with a solid-looking crystal glass turned upside down beside it. She turned over the glass and filled it with a rich reddish-brown liquid from the carafe. She brought it to her nose and sniffed experimentally. It smelled acrid and sweet, with a hint of fruitiness. "What is this?"

"Tuica. It's a locally brewed plum brandy. If you don't like it, I'll fetch you something else."

She sipped it cautiously, prepared for it to overwhelm her. Her limited experiences with foreign alcohols— Guinness and ouzo—hadn't led her to expect otherwise. Anca was surprised to find the flavor was crisp and refreshing, and the mouthful went down smoothly.

Next, she lifted the lid from the bowl and found some kind of soup with a dollop of sour cream on it. She swirled her spoon through the broth, seeing onions, carrots, zucchini, and dough balls. "And this, Demi?"

"*Bors de dovlecei*. It's sour soup with zucchini."

She nodded. Again, with caution, she took a spoonful and tasted it. She couldn't hide her grimace. Once she had swallowed it, Anca laid her spoon on the tray and covered the bowl.

She lifted the cover from the plate and was relieved to find the food semi-recognizable. She used her fork to indicate the vegetable dish. "I know this is eggplant, though I haven't seen it served this way."

"It's baked with garlic."

She nodded, moving her fork to the rolls that looked like miniature green burritos. "I'm not quite sure about this."

"Sarmale with vegetables and Mititei."

She smiled at him. "Translation, please?"

Demi chuckled, and the sound reminded her of the dream. "Romanian sausage and vegetables, wrapped with cabbage leaves. Sarmale is peppers or cabbage stuffed with anything."

Anca took a bite of the eggplant and closed her eyes with pleasure. It seemed to melt on her tongue, while the tang of garlic reinforced the more delicate seasonings. The sarmale was equally delicious, and she made short work of the meal, not even pausing for conversation. He seemed content to watch her, and she found his eyes constantly on her to be comforting instead of disconcerting.

When Anca pushed away her tray with a sigh, she said, "Thank you. I wouldn't have known what to order."

Demi inclined his head. "I live to serve you."

She jerked at the unexpected phrase, echoed from her dream. "What?" she demanded stridently.

He frowned. "Have I offended you?"

She crinkled the napkin still on her lap with her fingers. "What made you say that?"

Demi shrugged. "It's a common phrase in my country. People have been using it for thousands of years, in response to requests from the royal family."

Anca sighed with relief. He hadn't been mocking her dream. She must be losing her mind if she really believed he had somehow eavesdropped on the images parading through her brain during her nap. "I see…" She trailed off. "Do you work for the royal family?"

He hesitated, and then nodded. "In a manner of speaking. The king fostered me as a child. I have been," his brow wrinkled, as if he was searching for a way to explain, "adopted into the family, I guess you could say."

Anca nodded. "It must be a habit, huh?"

Demi looked confused. "Pardon, Anca?"

"To use that phrase." She grinned at him. "I'll have to remember it if we see any royalty during my visit."

His eyes widened, and he blinked several times. His mouth opened and closed, and he took a deep breath. Demi cleared his throat. "There has been confusion, I think."

"How so?"

"I live at Castle Draganescu, Anca. I serve your father, as do all Corsovan citizens. In return, he shepherds and guides us. He is the Protector of our way of life."

She shook her head, confused by his flowery speech. "I don't understand."

"Your father is the ruler of Corsova. Your mother is the queen, living in exile by her own choice. You are heir to the throne."

Silence filled the compartment as he stopped speaking. Anca knew her mouth had dropped open, but she couldn't seem to concentrate enough to close it. Her eyes felt as though they would bug out of their sockets. She shook her head. "Uh…"

"Anca?" His tone was full of concern.

She shook her head more vigorously. "That's crazy." There was a shrill edge to her voice, and she struggled to restrain it. "I'm not the heir to anything. I own a tea shop, for goodness' sakes."

Demi spread his hands apart in a gesture of helplessness. "That may be, but you are also the princess of Corsova, and the next in line for the throne." He frowned. "I can't believe Katrine never told you."

A sharp laugh escaped her. "Mother said my father was a shepherd." The laugh changed to a giggle that held a note of hysteria. "I guess she wasn't lying completely," Anca said when the urge to laugh faded.

His frown deepened. "I'm certain she had reasons for not telling you."

She shrugged, unable to come up with one or deal with what she had just learned.

"It's better you learn this now, no?"

"No!" She didn't have to hesitate. "I don't want this kind of burden. Jesus, Demi, don't you think it's stressful enough to meet my father for the first time, without knowing about this added BS?"

He shook his head. "BS?"

"Bullshit," she said very clearly.

"What does bull excrement have to do with the situation?"

The urge to laugh almost overwhelmed her again, but Anca feared her control was so tenuous that if she gave in, it would never stop. She would end up booked into a room at some Eastern European sanitarium. "Never mind," she said impatiently. "It's just a figure of speech."

"Ah."

Her eyes narrowed. "I hope you don't think I'm here to take over for my father, or some such nonsense. I don't want any part of this."

"But—"

Anca pressed on. "I've come to meet this Valdemeer, and then I'm going home. Back to New York, back to my mother, back to my shop, and back to my real life."

Demi scowled. "What of your duty to your people?"

"I have no people. The closest thing to 'my people' is the neighborhood watch program." She snorted. "I didn't know anything about this. If you'd been honest from the start, I wouldn't have come."

He stiffened, and his expression bordered on angry. "I did not lie to you. I assumed your mother had told you of your birthright. Do not blame me for this shock. I had nothing to do with siring you or stealing you from your people for twenty-seven years."

She swallowed. "I'm sorry," she said stiffly. "It's a shock, you know?"

He inclined his head, but his eyes still gleamed with anger. "I suggest you get over your shock. We will be in Bulgainia in ten minutes. It's another hour from there to Castle Draganescu. I'll expect you to be in control when you meet your father. He doesn't need to be upset the first night he finally gets to meet you."

Anca opened her mouth to protest.

"You can tell him of your objections later, but they should be directed toward him." Demi sighed. "The decision of whether or not you will have to assume your duties will rest with him."

She frowned at the stiffness in his tone. "Sorry to bother you." She couldn't hide the hint of hurt in her voice.

"It is no bother," he said distantly.

She nibbled on her lip, absurdly hurt at the barrier he seemed to be erecting between them. "Well, then..." She trailed off, unable to think of anything to add.

"If you would like to freshen up, the bathroom is down the hall. It is prominently marked with a female form."

She nodded and slid from the chair. She didn't look at Demi as she rushed from the compartment and down the hallway. It wasn't until she had locked herself into the small lavatory that she let her cool expression fade into one of blatant terror. Anca met her haunted brown eyes in the mirror and was amazed at how much green glowed in their depths. That only happened when she was emotional.

She ran a shaky hand through her fall of dark-brown hair, attempting to restore order to it after its dishevelment from her nap. Her thoughts weren't on making herself more presentable though. She couldn't stop thinking about Demi's revelation.

What did he want from her? More importantly, what did her father want from her? What if he refused to let her go home? If he were the king, would anyone defy him to help her leave the country?

A sinking feeling hit her stomach, and she bent forward. She started shaking, and tears burned in her eyes. She had to get home. What would become of her mother and *Dragan's Whimsy* if she didn't?

Anca took a deep breath and stood up slowly. She met her eyes in the mirror again and tried to force a reassuring smile. She just needed a plan.

Gradually, an idea formed in her mind. She played it out several times, until she heard the train whistle announcing they were approaching a stop. She examined herself from head to foot, pleased to see she appeared steady. Having a plan always calmed her.

She pasted on a slightly shaky smile and exited the ladies' room. Anca couldn't give Demi even a hint of what she planned if she hoped to succeed.

# Chapter Four

Anca walked near enough to Demi not to lose her way, but not so close as to allow him to easily reach out and grab her. She scanned the platform as they stepped off the train, and was shocked by the lack of activity. There were a few people milling about, but nothing like she had seen at Gara Constanta.

She took a step onto the old wood of the platform, and it creaked under her shoes. She turned her head to eye the station, built from gray stones, with a sloped roof. A board of schedules was posted on the outside, above the window where a clerk stood, but she didn't recognize the language.

Her attention turned to a small group hugging and crying near them. The boy they were embracing had tears shimmering in his eyes, but his posture was stiff. They faced the other set of tracks on the opposite side of the platform.

Demi must have seen her eyes on the other tracks, because he said, "The train turns around here at the capitol. It will make a circle a few miles out of town and head back to Gara Constanta."

She looked up at him, struggling to appear disinterested. "I see. So, it does that in a short time?"

He nodded. "Just a few minutes."

As he spoke, the train they had departed from headed down the tracks again.

Demi shifted the luggage to one arm and put his hand at her waist. "I left my car in the lot."

"Okay." She tensed as she felt his hand on her waist, but tried to hide her tension. Anca bit her lip, fretting over her plan. It had been contingent on her getting lost in a crowd, but there was no crowd here.

As they neared the family with the young man, Anca stepped closer to them. She knocked against his pile of luggage, sending it sprawling across the platform. She bit back a twinge of remorse when one of the cases opened and spilled its contents. She felt bad for the boy and wished she hadn't had to do that, but what choice did she have?

"Oh, I'm so sorry!" Anca exclaimed, clapping hands to her cheeks, as though hiding a blush. She turned to Demi. "We have to help."

The family was muttering, and the boy's hot glare fixed on her. As soon as Demi made apologies in their language, their angry expressions faded. He set down their cases and knelt to help gather their items.

Anca pretended to do the same, until Demi was kneeling with his back turned. She got up from her semi-crouch and sprinted across the platform. She could see a sheltering stand of trees in a field across the parking lot and pumped her legs for added speed. If she could make it to the trees, she would be able to hide until the train came back through.

Once on the train, Demi wouldn't be able to get her off it. There would be train employees and security to keep her safe. Surely, she could purchase her ticket on the train, or send one of the employees to do so for her. Once they realized she was in danger, of course.

Would Demi follow her? Anca knew he would, even as she asked herself the question. He appeared to be the loyal type and had promised her father he would bring her back with him. He wouldn't let her escape easily.

She plunged into the stand of trees as she heard the soles of his dress shoes skidding across the parking lot. Anca cursed the twilight sky, wishing for full darkness. She moved deeper into the stand of junipers and firs. They were old, and there was little room to maneuver between them. Their proximity hampered her movements, but it made for numerous hiding places.

She came to a thick clump of bushes sheltering a spot between two trees. Anca dropped to her knees and slithered through the bushes. She attempted to still them behind her, to cover her tracks.

She huddled on the wet ground, feeling cool mud soak into the knees of her pants. Anca struggled to control her ragged breathing. She held her breath when she heard a twig snap near her location.

She continued to hold her breath, straining to hear another telltale sound from Demi. She prayed the next one would be farther from her hiding place. Her heart raced, and her head was light. When she couldn't stand it anymore, Anca let out her breath in a low exhale. As she drew in another, she heard the rustle of leaves.

She cried out as Demi's arm reached into the bushes and lifted her out effortlessly. She tried to jerk free from his hold on her arm, and his grip tightened. She bent forward and sank her teeth into the back of his hand.

He stiffened, but made no move to let go of her.

Anca bit down harder, until the sharp tang of blood filled her mouth. She heard his breath hiss through his teeth, but it didn't sound like he was in pain.

A curious sensation swept through her as his blood flowed onto her tongue. Already light-headed, the forest seemed to spin around her. She attempted to move her mouth, but her teeth were hooked into his flesh.

Blood spurted into her mouth, and Anca swallowed it. The light-headed sensation faded, and a surge of renewed energy swept through her. She looked up at Demi through the veil of her lashes. He had thrown back his head, and he seemed to be in the throes of ecstasy.

With a frightened grasp, she tore her mouth free. Anca cried out when she saw the jagged tears in his skin. Her eyes fastened on the blood trickling down his hand, and she couldn't seem to pull her gaze from it. She whimpered when Demi brought his hand to his mouth and licked away the blood.

His eyes were dark with passion when he pulled her against him. His lips were anything but tender when they claimed hers. The kiss was hot and hungry—full of urgent needs and desires.

Anca pressed her body closer to his, parting her lips eagerly to accept his tongue. She stroked hers across his, wanting to taste every inch of him. His blood was on both of their tongues, and the scent and taste filled her senses. It was like the dream.

She pushed against his tongue, trying to push hers inside his mouth. She winced when her tongue raked across her teeth. Her canine tooth punctured her tongue, and the flash of pain brought her back to herself. Anca pushed against him as she became aware of their surroundings.

She stared up at him, trying to make out his expression in the deepening twilight, trying to pretend she hadn't just drank some of his blood and relished the experience. No! She hadn't enjoyed it. It had been an accident. Somehow, her teeth lodged in his skin, and when the blood flooded her mouth, she had swallowed without thought. His kiss had aroused her, not tasting his blood.

"Why did you run, Anca?" His voice was hoarse with passion, and his uninjured hand shook when he brought it up to smooth his hair.

She swallowed. "I changed my mind. Please let me go home."

"Valdemeer is expecting you." He sounded regretful. "I swore I would bring you back."

She began wringing her hands. "What if he won't let me go? I don't want to be a prisoner here."

Demi sighed. "Your father is a good man. He only wants what's best for you."

She wasn't reassured by his answer. "I want to go home. I don't want to worry about being an heir to a kingdom. I don't want to look over my shoulder all the time. This isn't the way I want my life to be."

His eyes burned with an inner light. "I will protect you with my life, Anca. Your father would do the same. You have nothing to fear." He touched her cheek gently. "Nothing happens without a purpose."

She frowned up at him dubiously. "You really believe that?"

"It is a tenant of our beliefs. Trust me. Come with me now and meet your father." He held out his hand.

Anca stared down at it, reluctant to accept his hand, but afraid not to. She didn't think he would hurt her. Her fear was deeper and less specific. Slowly, she raised her hand and grasped his. It felt as though the actions of her arm were independent from her body.

"Promise me you won't run away again?" There was a hint of steel in his voice.

"I..." She hesitated.

"I can't protect you if I don't know where you are. Promise me." He spoke firmly, and his eyes bored into hers.

She nodded. "I promise," she heard herself say weakly.

* * * * *

The castle came into sight as Demi's car topped the last hill. The road from the capitol to the castle was a long series of twisting curves, rising elevations, and poor roads. When she asked about the condition of the roads, Demi told her few people had vehicles, and the horses and wagons had little trouble with the rocky and uneven path.

She gasped softly when Castle Draganescu came into view. It was too dark to make out all the details, but she saw three pointed spires rising high into the sky.

Otherwise, the castle resembled a solid rectangle, with chimneys sprouting from the roof. It looked older than she could imagine, except for a rounded tower on the side that didn't quite mesh with the older style. The stone looked newer, and it had more of a baroque appearance than most traditional Eastern European castles.

"How old is it?" she asked with awe. Why had her mother walked away from all this? She had spent years working three jobs, and all that time she could have lived the life of a queen. Had it truly been necessary for Kathryn to turn her back on her home and position to protect her child?

"About a thousand-years-old." Demi pointed to the tower as they went down the hill. "Except the tower. It was added two hundred years ago."

Anca's eyebrows lifted when they neared the opened drawbridge. Two men in gray uniforms stood guard on each side of it. They waved Demi's car through with a brisk salute.

"Is this on the tour schedule?"

He glanced at her briefly as he pulled up near the smaller main entrance—though "smaller" was a relative term, since the wooden doors blocking entrance to the castle were at least ten-foot high. "Pardon?"

"You know, the tourist stops. You could probably make enough from admissions to pave the roads."

He shut off the engine and engaged the parking brake as the heavy doors creaked open, and four people scurried out to meet them. "We have no need—"

"Without cars, sure, but with an economic boost, everyone could afford cars."

He sighed. "Most of us are content with our way of life."

She sensed his annoyance with the topic and closed her mouth quickly to avoid offering any further unwanted advice. After all, what did she know of running a country? Nothing. Moreover, she wanted to keep it that way.

Before she could formulate an innocuous response, the passenger door opened, and a man was bowing to her. He wore simple trousers, a cotton shirt, and a quilted vest.

His garments could have fit well with any period in history during the last five hundred years. "Your Highness," he greeted obsequiously.

She almost looked over her shoulder before she remembered she was whom he addressed. It was disconcerting to go from plain Anca to something so pretentious. However, she restrained the urge to tell him to use her first name. She imagined the lack of protocol would shock him. "Hello," she said instead, with a shaky smile. When in Rome, er, Corsova...

He offered his hand to assist her from the car. She took it and slid out. He immediately dropped his light hold and bowed again.

"Thanks."

A woman who had remained a few steps away surged forward. She was middle-aged, with a heavy frame, curling gray-black hair, and a simple cotton tunic and pants. She curtsied with surprising grace, and her generous bosom threatened to spill from the top of her low-cut shirt. "Welcome, m'lady. His Majesty eagerly awaits news of your arrival."

"I'm here," she said, trying not to sound flustered. If the groveling was any indication of what she could expect for the next few days, she would go insane. Anca didn't realize how stiff she was until she felt the light touch of Demi's hand at her waist.

"This is Luiza, the cook." He turned slightly to the man who had greeted her. "This is Geza, the steward." He waved the other two servants nearer. The girl, with her thick, dark hair bound in a bun, curtsied when Demi's eyes rested on her. "Helena will be your personal attendant during your stay."

The other man bowed once at the waist when Demi turned to him. His eyes glinted with an unidentifiable emotion, and his expression was stern. "Petru is in charge of security here at the castle."

Anca didn't know whether to curtsey in return, incline her head imperiously, or ignore the greetings. In the end, she smiled and said a soft, "Hello."

Demi glanced down at the muddy knees of her slacks. "You will no doubt wish to change before meeting His Majesty. I will show you to your rooms." He nodded to Geza. "Please bring up the princess's luggage."

"Yes, m'lord."

Anca followed Demi into the castle, and she was pleasantly surprised to find electric lights. She had half-expected torches on the wall and candles in holders, judging from the time warp the rest of the country seemed to be stuck in.

As Demi led her through the castle, she absorbed it all with wide-eyed wonder. Threadbare tapestries hung on the walls, portraying people and events she assumed were from the history of the country. Her shoes made a clunking sound when the soles landed on the hard stone. An occasional fur or woven rug was scattered throughout the entryway.

Three large dogs napped near the fireplace. As they walked past them, the dogs lifted their heads and sniffed. Their eyes seemed more intelligent than any dog's she had ever seen, and she realized they were wolves. The smallest, palest brown one growled low in its throat, until the dark-brown wolf nudged it with its head. The palest one subsided into silence, though its gaze still seemed watchful.

Demi glanced over his shoulder. "Sorin, Lucian, and Starr. They are loyal to your family. When you win their trust, they will never leave you."

Anca nodded, pretending she wasn't terrified of the wolves behind her, and pretending she didn't think it was strange to have them as pets.

As they left the main chamber, dominated by the large table and a dozen sturdy chairs, Demi walked up a set of winding stone stairs. The wooden banister glowed, indicating years of care and use. She grabbed hold for support and found it smooth to the touch.

The stairs seemed to go on forever before they emerged onto the next landing. "This way." Demi walked down the hall and turned in front of a set of double doors. He pushed one open, and they stepped into a hall with another set of stairs. "Your wing is on the next floor."

Her eyes widened at the word wing. Never in her life had she had a room bigger than fourteen feet by fourteen feet. She followed him up the stairs—this set climbed straight up at a steep angle—and they stepped onto the third-floor seconds later. A dark-red rug, bordered with green and gold leaves, covered the expanse of the hallway.

Demi turned to the right, and Anca followed. He stopped before a massive set of dark mahogany doors farther down the hallway and twisted the gold handle. The door swung open without even a creak, and he stepped back to allow her to precede him.

She stepped into the chamber, finding it lit with the soft glow of a lamp on the mahogany nightstand. The bed was larger than any she had ever seen, and it was in a wooden frame with steps leading up to it. A black comforter covered the bed, and matching curtains hung from the posts of the bed frame. The rest of the furniture matched the nightstand—mahogany, sturdy, and polished to a high sheen.

Demi walked to a pair of doors against the far wall. He touched the nearest. "This is your dressing room." He moved his hand to the second. "The *en suite* bathroom. If you want to bathe, I'll return for you in one hour."

She nodded, overwhelmed with nerves at the thought of meeting her father. Would she hate him on sight? Would she revert to the child who wanted to scream all the angry words she had saved up during a lifetime of disappointments? Would she be able to forgive him?

Demi walked to the door, but he paused near a cord hanging from the ceiling. It looked like braided gold. "Ring for Helena if you need anything. Pull this once, and she'll come."

Anca nodded again. She watched as he stood by the door for another few seconds, seeming intent on speaking. Finally, he shook his head and left her without another word. He closed the door behind him.

She sagged as soon as she was alone. She was trembling, and focused on breathing deeply to calm herself. No matter how the meeting with her father turned out, it couldn't be as bad as she was imagining it. It was better to get herself in hand so she was prepared to meet him.

She glanced down at her soiled outfit and grimaced. It wouldn't do to wear such an outfit for an audience with the king. By the time Anca bathed, her cases would be in her room. A hot bath might be just the thing to sooth her ragged nerves. Maybe several baths, as frazzled as she was right then. It wouldn't hurt if Demi joined her, to wash her back.

She swallowed down a moan as the erotic thought translated to an even more erotic image in her mind. She couldn't recall ever having been drawn to someone so quickly in her life. Her two casual affairs had been born more from a reaction to the peer pressure of her girlfriends in college than any real interest on her part, and both had been less than satisfying.

Adam, her first, had lasted all of two weeks, and then he had gone onto a girl who was more enthusiastic. The relationship had ended so quickly Anca hadn't realized they never clicked on a level beyond physical until she analyzed it years later, after Barry.

The sex had been nice with Barry, boyfriend-number-two, but there had been a vital emotional connection missing. She had never felt like she really knew him, and vice versa. They had both tried hard to make it work, but at the nine-month mark, when he pressed for a deeper commitment and gave her a ring, she had walked away.

So it was alarming to feel this physical and emotional connection with Demi after such a short acquaintance. For the last three years, she had believed she would never find anyone who suited her, so it should be a relief to know she could connect with a man.

It would have been, if he didn't live halfway around the world. If only he had been a New Yorker, and they met on the subway, she would be rejoicing. She probably would have taken him to her bed at their first meeting under those circumstances.

Here in Corsova, it wasn't safe to give into her desires. If she fell in love with him, she would have a hell of a time walking away. Without having to feel him out, Anca knew Demi would never leave his country, and she wouldn't be content to stay.

Another doomed relationship, she thought with a sigh, as she walked into the bathroom. She must have the magical touch where men were concerned.

As she took in the grandeur of the bathroom half-heartedly, she tried telling herself she was worrying for nothing. She knew he was attracted to her too, but that didn't mean he was looking for a commitment. He would probably run away if he knew how serious her thoughts were. He might be involved with someone or married.

She remembered the feel of his mouth on hers—in the dream and real life—and the way his heart raced when he held her earlier. The earnestness in his vow to protect her came back to her, and Anca knew he wanted her with equal fervor. Based on the other qualities he had displayed, that ruled out the possibility he was already in a relationship, meaning he was available.

Which was why she would have to keep her distance, she decided. One of them would have to be sensible, and she didn't think Demi was sitting around agonizing about his growing attraction for her. Being sensible fell to her. Too bad she wasn't so good at being sensible in her personal life.

# Chapter Five

Nikia squirmed as the tongue in her pussy probed deeper. She arched her hips, bringing her clit more fully against Sian's tongue. She dug her hands into her lover's long hair, pushing her face deeper into the crux of her legs. She groaned as Sian's teeth raked across her swollen clit.

She was so engrossed in what was happening in her pussy that she didn't hear the door opening. She didn't open her brown eyes until the door slammed shut. She grimaced when she saw the cowering posture of the servant. As the silence lengthened, she propped herself on her elbows. "Did you have some reason to disturb me without knocking, Helena?"

The girl nodded slowly.

"Well, spit it out," she snapped.

Helena bobbed into a curtsey. "She's here, m'lady."

With a snarl of rage, Nikia rolled out of bed. She snatched her robe from where it lay over the footboard and thrust her arms into it so violently the delicate silk shredded under the onslaught of her fingernails. "That bastard."

"Who, m'lady?" Helena's dark eyes clearly reflected her confusion.

"Nicodemus. How dare he bring her here?" Her eyes narrowed. "Stupid bitch. She'll be sorry she came." She turned her head as Sian moved from the bed. She lunged forward and buried her hands in the other woman's hair.

Nikia dragged her from the bed, ignoring her cry of pain when her knees hit the stone floor with a dull thud. "You aren't finished," she hissed.

As Sian knelt before her and returned her mouth to her pussy, Nikia beckoned the young maid closer. She didn't miss the girl's hesitation, and the fear only added to her ire. When Helena was close enough, she slapped her. "Be quick when I summon you."

Tears sparkled in her eyes, and she cupped her cheek as she nodded.

"Have you seen her?"

"Yes, m'lady. Sian's mother says she's the very image of Katrine." She bowed her head. "I've been assigned to serve her." She cringed, bringing her arms up to shield her face, evidently expecting a reprimand.

Instead, Nikia caressed her cheek, the same one she had slapped. "Excellent. You'll keep an eye on the bitch-princess for me, until I can deal with her."

"Yes, m'lady." She sounded uncertain as she lowered her arms.

Nikia tangled her hand in the girl's tightly bound hair, pulling her closer. When her lips were near Helena's, she whispered, "Serve the wench, but remember who your mistress is."

Helena swallowed audibly. "O-of course, m'lady."

She stiffened as Sian's tongue brought her to orgasm. Nikia's fingernails dug into the young girl's flesh, and she smiled when Helena winced. She bucked her hips against Sian's face, and slowly the pleasure faded.

She pulled Helena closer, pressing her mouth to the soft, full lips of the young woman. Nikia ignored her resistance. She kept the kiss light and soon lifted her head.

Her eyes bored into Helena's. "You belong to me, don't you, Helena?"

Tears splashed down her cheeks as she nodded.

"Good girl." She dropped her hand from behind Helena's head and brought her fingers to her mouth. She licked away all traces of the blood she'd drawn. Then she looked down at Sian, who awaited permission to leave her post. "You may rise. I suddenly have the urge to dine with my dear father. Help me prepare."

Sian got up from the floor and rushed into the bathroom. The sound of running water soon reached the bedroom.

She turned toward the bathroom, but stopped in mid-step. She turned her head to look at Helena. "Be sure your service pleases me, girl."

Helena nodded. "I live to serve you, m'lady." Her voice was shaky as she repeated the ancient phrase.

She licked her lips, eyeing the girl's full bosom. "Not yet, but soon." She swept into the bathroom, leaving the girl behind her. She could sense her fear and reluctance, and it aroused her again. No conquest was so sweet as one who started out unwilling.

She dropped the robe and stepped into the bath. Bubbles frothed on the surface of the water and hid her breasts when she leaned back in the spacious tub. Sian perched on the rim of the tub, holding a natural sponge. She smiled at her, while imagining how sweet Helena's pussy would taste. Sian's neediness was growing tiresome, and she was ready for a change.

Once she did away with Valdemeer's heir and ridded herself of the old man, she would celebrate her ascension by inaugurating the young woman as her new companion.

If the girl resisted, so much the better. She got wet just thinking about forcing Helena into compliance.

As Sian stepped into the tub and knelt between her legs, Nikia leaned back. The first touch of the sponge against her inflamed pussy was rough, but it only enhanced her desire.

Sian's fingers were gentle as they parted her pussy lips. She swirled the sponge against her clit, and Nikia groaned. Her nipples ached for attention, and she cupped her breasts with her own hands. She traced her fingers across her areole, flicking her nipples gently.

Sian plunged her fingers deep inside Nikia's dripping pussy. As she did so, Nikia twisted her nipples almost viciously, fantasizing they were her half-sister's neck.

# Chapter Six

Demi bowed to Valdemeer, standing by the mini-bar, before taking a seat in the wingchair across the desk. "Good evening, sire."

Valdemeer poured him a glass of cognac without asking. He put it on the edge of the desk before sitting in his chair behind the desk. "She is here?"

He lifted the crystal glass to sip the cognac before answering. "Yes, sire."

"And your journey? Was it…uneventful?"

Demi hesitated over mentioning Anca's attempted escape. He sighed. "She grew frightened upon learning she is your heir."

Valdemeer's gray brows formed a V. "She didn't know?"

"No, sire."

He stroked his beard, looking thoughtful. "What does she know of us, Nicodemus?"

"I don't think she knows anything, sire. Katrine told her you had died, and that she was a Ukrainian immigrant."

The king swallowed heavily. "I see." He glanced down at the amber liquid in his glass, seeming to collect his thoughts. "How is Katrine?"

He set down the glass. "She's been ill. She's had heart surgery, and Anca said she's fragile."

He shook his head. "How can that be? She's so young."

"I don't think she lives by our ways any longer, sire. She has become human."

Valdemeer leaned back in his chair, looking troubled. "Anca knows nothing of what we are? What she is?"

"I don't think so."

He stroked his graying beard again. "Damned impossible position, eh, boy?"

Demi smiled at the unintentional use of the endearment. "Yes, sire."

"How should I tell her? Can she deal with it all upfront?"

He hesitated, and then shrugged. "I don't know. She seems to be resilient, but it isn't exactly the kind of thing you blurt out over dinner, is it?"

"No, I suppose it isn't." Valdemeer shook his head. "How would you handle it?"

"I really can't say—"

"Nonsense, Nicodemus. You know more about her than any of us, except maybe Ylenia. You have a stake in how this happens. Tell me what I should do."

"I think you should ease her into acceptance. Don't rush her. She's already had several surprises in the past few days."

Valdemeer grimaced. "Difficult to do, with time growing short. The blood-moon is only a few weeks away."

Demi shrugged. "You asked my opinion, sire."

His king nodded. "Yes, I did. I suppose you're right." He leaned forward, slapping his hands together with a meaty thud. "Tonight, I won't mention it. I deserve a chance to get acquainted with my daughter for the next few days, before we have to talk about her future."

"Yes, sire." He wondered if Anca would let the discussion wait though. She was terrified of her father trying to keep her in Corsova. Would that cause her to speak up, or would she be careful and discreet?

Valdemeer nodded, and he seemed more energized. "Go fetch her, dear boy. After waiting so long, I can't wait another moment to lay eyes on my daughter."

Demi rose from his chair. "I live to serve you."

Valdemeer chuckled. "How many times do I have to tell you not to say that, Nicodemus? You're a member of the family."

"But, sire…"

His dark eyes twinkled. "Or you will be."

Demi swallowed down his nausea as nerves assailed him. "If she'll have me."

\* \* \* \* \*

Anca attempted to steady her shaking hands as she followed Demi into a lavish sitting room. She didn't think the Persian carpet was imitation, nor were the Chippendale chairs knockoffs. She focused solely on the ormolu clock on the mantle for a few seconds, struggling to remember how to breathe.

When she felt calmer, Anca turned slightly to face the man standing in the corner of the room, near a mini-bar. Her father. She could barely fathom that. She stood frozen to the spot as she stared at him.

He had long, dark hair secured in a leather thong. Strands of silver liberally streaked his hair. Dark eyes dominated his chiseled features. His skin bore wrinkles as testament to his age, but he looked handsome and vital. His posture was straight, and his shoulders were broad. He didn't look sick.

He was staring at her just as intently. Silence reigned in the salon for long seconds, until he broke it with a harsh exhalation. He stepped toward her, and his eyes shone with unshed tears. "You are your mother." He smiled. "I can almost believe Katrine is standing before me."

"I have your nose," Anca said, and her voice emerged as a croak. She had always wondered where it came from, since it was straight and narrow, unlike her mother's pert little nose. She touched it unconsciously, while staring at his. She saw a tear slide down his cheek and realized her own cheeks were wet.

Later, she wouldn't remember who moved first. When thinking about it, all she could recall was the feel of her father's arms embracing her in a hug that was twenty-six years past due.

He smelled of cognac, pine, and a trace scent of copper. His beard was rough where it pressed against the top of her head. The scratchy material of his tunic tickled her skin when she buried her face in it and sobbed. He murmured words in a language she didn't understand as he stroked her hair.

For a moment, Anca forgot about everything, even Demi's presence. She was too overwhelmed with emotions to suppress the harsh sobs. She rubbed her cheek against his shirt, allowing his soothing tone to wash over her. Slowly, the tears lessened and dried up.

She lifted her head and gazed into her father's eyes. She blurted out the question on her mind without thought. "Why didn't you come after me?"

Valdemeer flinched, and a hint of color swept into his pale cheeks. His hand in her hair stilled. "I wanted to." He shook his head. "You were safer in New York."

She swallowed a lump of moisture in her throat. "Demi told me that. I don't understand why you couldn't at least come see me in New York. Why pretend I didn't exist for twenty-six years?"

"Never that, dear daughter." He shook his head. "It is complicated."

Anca blinked back another round of tears at his vague answer. She could continue prodding him for information she didn't think he would give, or she could ease off and spend the next few days becoming acquainted with him. Surely, he would tell her everything before she left.

She nodded. "I see." To her surprise, he kissed her forehead, tickling her skin with his beard and mustache.

"I promise I will give you an explanation soon, Anca. Tonight, I want only to enjoy your company and learn more about you."

She nodded again and stepped away from him. For a second, the physical separation seemed to span miles. She forced a shaky smile. "All right...Papa," She said the name hesitantly. When Kathryn spoke of him, she had always called him her Papa. It had become second nature to think of him that way.

Would he think it was too soon? Was it too soon to be calling him Papa? Part of her rebelled at her easy acceptance of the man standing before her. Too much time had passed, and they would never recover it. He had wounded her deeply with his rejection, whether or not it was intentional.

Yet, Anca felt an instant connection with her father. He had felt it too. She was certain he had. A week ago, she had accepted never knowing her father. Now that she knew differently and had a chance to know him, she didn't want to waste it by imposing needless barriers and giving life to resentments accrued during a fatherless childhood.

She held her breath, awaiting his reaction. Her stomach clenched as the ticking of the clock seemed to grow louder. She was near apologizing for being so forward when he gathered her in his arms again and hugged her with bone-crushing strength.

When he released her, he didn't say anything about it. He seemed to be determined to ignore the tears clinging to his lashes. Valdemeer cleared his throat. "Dinner is waiting." He held out his arm.

Anca linked hers through his and walked with him through the salon. Her eyes locked with Demi's as they passed him, and she gave him a small smile. She tried to say, "Thank you," with her eyes. If he hadn't come after her, she never would have known about her father.

As he fell in step behind them, his breath caressed her neck. "You're welcome," he whispered.

Her eyes widened. He had interpreted her thoughts just from her expression. A shiver raced up her spine. Demi seemed to know her intimately. How could that be? Was there such a thing as love at first sight, or was it just an instant attraction for both of them?

She was distracted from her thoughts as they entered the dining room. It was resplendent, with ecru silk wall hangings, thick carpets, and a cherry-stained, rectangle table long enough to seat thirty. Chippendale chairs lined each side of the table. Someone occupied the chair at the head of the table.

A stunning woman with cinnamon-red hair slid from the cushioned chair. She wore a flowing ebony caftan that did little to hide the voluptuous curves of her body. Her skin was olive, and her brown eyes glittered with green specks as she walked toward them. She seemed familiar, yet alien.

"Papa." The smile that flashed across her face did nothing to soften her hard expression. "I had heard your other child arrived."

Valdemeer inclined his head in Anca's direction. "This is Anca."

Anca swallowed heavily as those disconcerting eyes — so much like her own, she realized with a start — met hers. She forced a smile. "Hello."

The older woman stepped closer, stopping just a few inches away. She held out her hands. "Anca, my dear sister."

Anca's eyes widened. She didn't protest as the other woman folded her hands in a tight grip. "S-s-sister?"

She nodded. "Am I a surprise?" She looked sad. "Mother didn't tell you?"

How could her mother not tell her she had a sister? How could Kathryn have left her other daughter behind when she fled Corsova? What about protecting her too? Anca opened her mouth, but she couldn't find anything to say.

Demi stepped forward, and again, it was as if he sensed her thoughts. More likely, he sensed her tension. "This is Nikia, your *half*-sister. Katrine wasn't her mother."

"That's a beautiful name." She shook her head at the inane comment. What did one say to a sister she hadn't known about?

Nikia nodded. "It was my mother's choice. She insisted I have it. That was the last thing she said before she died." She spoke matter-of-factly, but her eyes darted to Valdemeer and stayed on him for a long second. "She was so young."

Anca frowned as the undercurrent of tension permeating the room suddenly increased. "I...uh, I'm sorry for your loss."

Nikia shrugged. "It was long ago, and I never knew her. Papa did though." There was a hint of slyness in her gaze. "He was there when she died so...unexpectedly."

"Women still die in childbirth," Valdemeer said stiffly. "Given Illiana's state, it wasn't entirely unexpected."

Nikia nodded, but she didn't dispute her father's words, as she so obviously wanted to. Instead, she leaned forward and kissed Anca's left cheek, and then her right cheek. "Welcome to the family, sister."

"Thank you." She pulled her hands free from her sister's hold, resisting the urge to wipe them on her linen slacks. There was something insincere about her façade, and Anca had the irrational urge to wash her hands to cleanse them from Nikia's touch.

Demi cleared his throat. "Shall we sit?"

Anca waited until Valdemeer and Nikia selected seats before she walked to the one on her father's left. She smiled at Demi as he held the chair for her before taking the seat beside her.

She was bursting with questions, but she was reluctant to voice any with Nikia present. Something in the woman's eyes paralyzed her tongue. Nikia was dangerous.

She blinked at the strange thought, wondering where it came from. It hadn't felt like a thought that flowed from her mind naturally. Rather, it had seemed to hammer its way into her thoughts abruptly.

Nikia was the first to break the awkward silence once the servants filled golden goblets with dark-red wine and placed soup before Anca, Demi, and Nikia. "How is your mother?" The question was appropriate, but there was a sharp edge to her tone. "Is she still living?"

"Yes. She's been ill."

"Her heart?" Nikia asked blandly.

Anca's eyes widened. "How did you know?"

She lifted a thin shoulder. "One of the servants mentioned your mother's condition."

She glanced at Demi with a frown. "News travels fast here, doesn't it?"

"Exceedingly." Nikia drained her glass and gestured to Geza, who stood by the doorway. He hurried forward to fill her glass again. "Will she recover?"

"If she avoids stress and follows her doctor's orders."

"It would be unfortunate if you returned to New York to find she had passed away during your vacation." Nikia clicked her tongue softly. "You mustn't tarry long here at Castle Draganescu."

"She isn't that ill." Anca's brow furrowed. Was she imagining the trace of warning she heard in her sister's voice?

Demi spoke up in a firm tone. "Nothing will happen to Her Highness. His Majesty instructed me to leave a guard with her while Anca was away, to ensure her well-being. They will have arrived by now." His eyes locked with Nikia's, and there seemed to be a battle of wills.

Finally, Nikia blinked. "That is good news." She set down her goblet and pushed away from the table. "If you'll excuse me, I have no appetite this evening." She nodded to Valdemeer and Demi before walking around the table to stand beside Anca.

Anca turned her head and looked up at her sister, feeling the tiny hairs on the back of her neck prickle with fear. She flinched as Nikia caressed her hair. She arched her neck, seeking to escape her sister's touch. She winced as Nikia's nails dug into her scalp, restricting her movement.

"It was lovely to meet you, sister." Nikia bowed her head and pressed her lips against Anca's in a soft kiss. Then she lifted her head and stepped away. She walked out of the dining room without looking back.

Anca stared after her sister, disconcerted. Nikia's parting hadn't seemed very...sisterly. She was distracted when Demi touched her thigh. She smiled at him, struggling not to show her confusion.

"Pay Nikia little mind," he said soothingly. "She's a turbulent woman."

Valdemeer sighed. "She's jealous of you, Anca."

She turned her head in her father's direction, noting Demi's hand remained on her thigh. As he stroked in slow circles, frissons of awareness darted through her leg. She shook her head. "That makes no sense."

If either of them had reason to be jealous, it was she. After all, Nikia had lived with their father all her life, and had obviously lived in luxury. She was a princess. It was doubtful she had ever wanted for anything in her childhood, except maybe a mother. That was enough to kill any envy Anca might feel, because she had a loving mother.

He sighed again, more deeply this time. He toyed with the stem of his goblet, but he didn't lift the cup to his mouth to drink. "She is upset because she wasn't chosen to be my heir."

"Is that all?" Anca shrugged. "You might as well know I'm not interested in the job, Papa. She can have it, as far as I'm concerned."

He hesitated, and his eyes narrowed. He exchanged looks with Demi. When he spoke, he apparently chose to disregard her statement of disinterest. "It is impossible for Nikia to inherit the Protectorate of Corsova. She was not born at the proper time."

Her eyes widened, and she read between the lines. "So, uh, you weren't married to her mother, huh?"

Valdemeer appeared startled, but he nodded. "Don't trouble yourself with Nikia," he said dismissively. "I'll deal with her."

Anca was rattled by the way her father's eyes darkened. She could sense his and Demi's mounting tension and was determined not to continue the conversation. As she searched her mind for a safer topic, she reached for the wine.

She took a sip and choked. It was thick and cloying, with a metallic taste. She reached for the linen napkin under the heavy silver cutlery, quickly wiping away the thick red liquid leaking down her chin. "I'm sorry." She could feel her cheeks heat with embarrassment.

Valdemeer gestured to Geza. "Bring Anca water immediately. She isn't accustomed to our native wine."

She nodded. Within seconds, a crystal goblet of iced water appeared before her, and she drank deeply.

"It takes some getting used to," Demi said, as she lowered the goblet. "Corsovan wine is more…robust than traditional vintages."

She nodded, but didn't respond. Robust was one way to describe it, she supposed. To her, it was more than robust. Corsovan wine tasted a lot like blood.

As the meal progressed, Anca fought back yawn after yawn. The days of travel had caught up with her, and she could barely keep open her eyes. She struggled to uphold her end of the conversation and answer Valdemeer's seemingly never-ending stream of questions, but it got more difficult to form coherent answers.

He must have realized, because he pushed away his untouched plate and nodded to Demi. "Nicodemus will see you to your room now, Anca. If you're inclined tomorrow evening before dinner, we'll play a game of chess. I would like to see if you remember anything from your school club."

Anca smothered a yawn with her hand and nodded. "It's been years since I had time for a game. I'd like to give it a try."

"Excellent."

Demi stood up and pulled out her chair. "Come."

She stood up, laying her napkin beside her almost full plate. The snack Demi brought her on the train had stuck with her. Coupled with her mounting exhaustion, she hadn't had much of an appetite. Only Demi had done justice to the vegetables and lamb. "I'll see you at breakfast, Papa."

He shook his head. "I keep odd hours, Anca. It will be the evening before I'll be free."

"Okay." Impulsively, she walked to his seat and leaned down to kiss his cheek. "Goodnight, Papa."

He touched her hand on his shoulder, squeezing gently. "Goodnight, *copia*."

"Child," Demi translated in a whisper.

She stood up and followed Demi from the dining room and through the castle. Instead of learning the route to her room, she focused on the way his buttocks flexed in the tailored slacks.

A hint of alertness returned as some of her sleepiness ebbed, replaced by a stirring of sexual tension. Her body ached for his. Common sense didn't offer much of a barrier to her desire. All the reasons she had thought of earlier to avoid getting involved with Demi seemed less important now.

She was so intent on her thoughts that she didn't pay attention when Demi stopped moving and turned in her direction. She walked right into him before she could stop herself. Her breath escaped with a sigh as his arms came around her to steady her.

He was frowning down at her. "Are you all right, Anca?"

She nodded. Her stomach tightened, and she licked her lips. "Fine, Demi." She shifted her weight from one foot to the other, which caused her chest to brush more fully against his. She put her hands on his chest. "Just fine," she said in a husky whisper.

He cleared his throat. "Well..." He trailed off as his eyes met hers.

Anca stared up at him, enchanted by the ruddy color in his cheeks. As she licked her lips again, with deliberate slowness this time, his cock hardened and pressed into her hip. She wriggled against him, smiling when he cupped his hands around her buttocks and pulled her lower body closer to his.

"What game are you playing?" he growled.

She shrugged as she moved her hand up to the back of his neck and twirled a lock of his hair around her finger. "I don't know," she said honestly. "I don't think it's a game." She cuddled closer. "I want you, Demi. I felt it the moment I touched you. I *saw* us making love that night in my shop."

He made a sound of frustration. "It's too soon, *meu dragostia*."

"*Meu dragostia*?" she repeated with confusion. "What's that?"

"It's Corsovan."

Anca rolled her eyes. "Of course it is. What does it mean?"

"It was a slip of the tongue." Demi shook his head. "I should leave you to sleep."

She shook her head. "Tell me what it means."

He sighed. "It would be best—"

Anca yanked gently on his hair. "I'll just ask someone else if you don't tell me."

Demi's mouth tightened. "Very well. It means 'my love'. Are you satisfied now?" His face flushed a brilliant scarlet, and he refused to meet her eyes.

She blinked at the telling statement, and his even more revealing reaction. "You felt it too."

He cursed. "I've always felt it, Anca. I've known you were my destined lifemate since before you were born. All my life, I've been prepared..." He trailed off, shaking his head. "Never mind."

She frowned at him. "What? I don't understand."

He eased her away from him. "Don't ask me to explain it all. That duty falls to your father or Ylenia."

Anca's head spun as she tried to absorb everything he said. "Please, I don't understand what you mean, Demi. What's a destined lifemate, and who is Ylenia? Is she my father's mistress?"

Demi scowled. "Ylenia is the spiritual guide of our people. She will tell you what you need to know." His expression hardened, and he dipped his head. "Good night." He turned away from her.

Before he took a step, Anca put her hand on his arm. "Wait." He stiffened, but he didn't move forward. "I'm only trying to understand. Everything is so different here." She took a deep breath, suppressing the sob that wanted to emerge. She was appalled at the urge to cry and blamed it on jet lag. "Everything has changed in the last three days. My only constant has been you. Don't leave me."

Slowly, Demi turned back to face her. His hand trembled when he stroked her cheek. "I will always be here for you."

She bit her lip, overwhelmed by the tenderness in his expression. "Am I truly your love, Demi?"

This time, there wasn't a hint of embarrassment in his expression. "Yes. I love you, Anca."

A tangle of conflicting emotions whirled through her. Pleasure at his words, mingled with fear. What did he expect from her? In New York, if a man she had known three days told her he loved her, she would run away as fast as she could. She would write him off as another crazy and move on.

She didn't doubt Demi's sanity or sincerity. Looking deep into his dark eyes, she could see the honest emotions reflected back. More than that, she could feel his love emanating from him in waves. She could almost see it and wondered if being in Corsova had honed her psychic abilities.

"I don't expect you to love me." His voice was hoarse, but he spoke levelly. "I didn't plan to tell you anything yet."

"Why not?" She bowed her head. "Are you ashamed of loving me?"

"Never," he said forcefully, "but you must choose me." With a gentle hand, he nudged up her chin. "It wasn't my place to burden you with my emotions."

She shook her head. "I don't understand. If we're destined to be together…" She trailed off, unable to accept so absurd a concept. Sure, she was attracted to him, and felt a deeper emotional connection with him than any man in her past, but destined lifemates? What an archaic concept. It was almost as ridiculous as arranged marriages.

"Destiny orchestrates what should be, but no one can force love if none is felt." He stroked her cheek. "We must all be free to choose what our heart wants."

She swallowed. "You've chosen me, have you?" She winced at the hint of skepticism in her tone.

He didn't seem offended. "I was certain we belonged together, but meeting you removed my last trace of doubt." Demi sighed. "You haven't been raised as I have, to expect our union. This is too much to spring on you. Rest now, and we'll talk later—whenever you're ready."

Once again, he moved to step away from her, but Anca locked her arms around his neck. "Don't leave."

"But—"

"Come inside with me." She laid her cheek on his chest. "I won't pressure you to talk about anything, if you don't want to."

"What do you want from me?" He sounded confused, not annoyed.

"Just hold me, Demi." Anca held her breath, waiting to see if he would agree. Again, she wondered what had happened to her decision to be sensible and avoid any deepening relationship with him. Perhaps she was just emotionally overwrought from meeting her father and longed for comfort. Anyone would do.

*Liar*, her heart whispered.

"If that's what you want," he said after a long pause.

"Yes," she whispered. She dropped her arms and took his hand to lead him through the wooden doors. As he fell in step behind her, she knew what had happened to her previous plan. His complete forthrightness about his feelings had left her without defenses. Before his revelation, she had wanted him, but now, her desire was even more intense.

As they entered the chambers assigned to her, Anca sensed the night ahead would change everything. The thought frightened her, but it was also exhilarating. Giving herself to Demi seemed like the most natural thing in the world, and she forgot about her fears as he closed the door behind them and took her into his arms.

# Chapter Seven

Demi held her against his chest without speaking or moving. Anca could hear the rhythm of his heartbeat echoing through her ear, until it mingled with her own inside her head. She closed her eyes and let him support her. She yearned for his touch, but having him hold her was almost enough.

She changed her mind when he nudged up her chin and claimed her lips. At five-eight, she was tall, but he still topped her by half a foot. He had to dip his head to kiss her, and she stretched her spine to meet him.

His lips were soft against hers, coaxing her into responding to his touch, but never demanding. He traced the plump contour of her lower lips with his tongue, and she buried her fingers in his blond hair. Anca parted her lips to urge his tongue inside, but he ignored the invitation.

Instead, he trailed his tongue down her chin to her neck. She closed her eyes and tipped her head backward as he breathed a trail across the column of her throat, to the bend of her neck where it met her shoulder. She pressed her lower body more firmly against his as he opened his mouth and breathed against her skin.

Her nipples hardened as his breath caressed her skin. She parted her legs and thrust her hips forward so she could straddle his thigh with her pussy. She rubbed it against his leg.

Demi flicked his tongue across her skin in teasing darts as one of his hands moved past her hips. He cupped her buttocks and lifted her more fully onto his leg.

Anca gyrated her hips and cried out as Demi nipped her neck. Her pussy tightened, and she moved her arms to lock them around his neck. Her legs were weak, and she didn't think she could stand at all without his assistance.

He moved both of his hands to her hips and lifted her into his arms. "Lock your legs around me," he said when he lifted his head.

Anca anchored both thighs around his waist. Her eyes widened as he moved to the writing table instead of the bed. As he set her on her feet beside it, she recognized the table from the vision she'd had of the two of them the night she met Demi.

He stepped away a few inches so he had room to strip off his light-blue button-down shirt. Anca's hands went to the hem of the red sweater she wore, but his hands covered hers.

"Let me." His voice was husky, and his cheeks had flushed pink. "I want to reveal you an inch at a time."

She let her hands drop to her sides. Anca waited for him to make the next move.

Demi dropped to his knees as he pushed up the sweater to her midriff. He buried his face in the flesh of her stomach and, once again, teased her with quick flicks of his tongue.

Anca anchored her hands in his hair, as her pussy grew more slippery with her arousal. Her body reacted instinctively to his proximity, preparing for his mouth to explore her pussy.

Instead, Demi moved upward, slowly rising from his knees as he pushed up the sweater and followed its path with his mouth.

She raised her arms for him to pull it off, and then stood in front of him in her pants and bra. Anca's swollen breasts pushed against the cups of her red bra, and her nipples were so hard they ached. "Please," she whispered, cupping one of her breasts in her hand, offering it to him. She traced the outline of the nipple with her finger.

Demi moaned, and his hands shook when he pushed the straps down her shoulders. His hands moved to her breasts. He paused briefly to touch the pendant nestled in the valley of her breasts. It glowed with golden glints. His fingers stroked it reverently before he returned his attention to her breasts.

Anca started to release her breast, but Demi cupped his hand around hers, pushing her hand more firmly into her soft flesh.

"What do you feel?"

She bit her lip, struggling to form coherent words as his other hand stroked her neglected breast through the silk cup. When he tweaked her nipple, she almost forgot how to speak. It was only when he pressed her fingers against her nipple again that she remembered his question.

"Pleasure," she said with a moan.

Demi shook his head. "How does your breast feel?"

She closed her eyes to capture a description. "Soft, but firm." Her voice was low, and she wondered if he could hear her. He circled her hand around her breast. "The bra is silky. It feels good rubbing against my nipple."

Demi moved her palm to cup the tip of her breast. "The nipple, Anca?"

"It's tingling with need."

He chuckled. "What does it need?" As he asked the question, he pushed down the cup on her other breast and stroked her nipple with his thumb and forefinger.

Anca groaned. "That," she managed to force out. "You."

He released her hand, letting it fall to her side. His fingers were steady when they moved to the clasp at her back and unfastened the bra. He pulled it away slowly and tossed it over his shoulder to join the sweater.

Her breasts were barely exposed before his hands replaced the bra and covered them. Each callous on his hands pressed into her soft flesh, exciting her nerve endings. He pushed his thumbs against her nipples with enough pressure to cause her pussy to spasm, but not enough to hurt. He moved his thumbs in slow circles, brushing the rough skin of his pads against her sensitive peaks.

Anca couldn't hold back a cry of pleasure. She couldn't summon the ability to care if a servant heard them making love.

Remembering the vision, she arched backwards until her back touched the writing table. Within seconds, Demi's mouth followed. He pressed his lips into the valley of her breasts and opened his mouth. He swirled his tongue over her skin, and she whimpered, begging him without words to touch her throbbing nipples with his tongue.

"Impatient," he said tenderly and moved his mouth to her right breast as he cupped her other breast in his hand.

He laved the turgid peak as he applied gentle pressure with his fingers to the other bud. His tongue moved in circles over her areole, moving outward and away from her nipple before swooping back in.

Anca groaned as he bit down gently on her nipple, while squeezing the other one with enough pressure to almost hurt. It didn't hurt though. It only made her aware of how sensitive her breasts were, and how neglected her pussy felt.

He seemed to read her thoughts, because his right hand moved from her hip to the waistband of her slacks. He undid the button and zipper in two quick motions, and then slid his hand inside the waistband, over her silk panties.

Anca's pussy spasmed as he stroked her lips through the silk panties. She was dripping with need, and thrust her hips upward, bringing her pussy more fully against his hand. She bit her lip to restrain a cry as he suckled on her nipple and pressed his fingers into her cleft, using the silk for added friction.

Demi moved his head from her breast to her mouth, forming a seal around her lips with his as he massaged her clit through the silk. He swallowed each of her tiny cries of pleasure as his finger explored her wet pussy through the flimsy barrier.

He slipped his hand from her breast to her navel, then lower. He pressed gently against the top of her pussy as he fingered her clit with increasing pressure.

Anca continued to arch against him. She tried to meet each stroke of his tongue on hers with one of her own, but she wasn't able to concentrate. Everywhere he touched her, he left behind a fire, and she was about to explode.

Frissons of awareness flashed from her nipples to her pussy, heightening her pleasure at his touch.

Demi's hand moved from the top of her pussy to the waistband of her pants. He pushed them down a few inches, one side at a time, without breaking the rhythm of his fingers in her pussy. With her pants lower, he had more room to maneuver, and he cupped her pussy in his hand.

Anca ground her pussy against his palm as he pressed upward in a partially circular motion. He kept up steadily increasing pressure as she continued to arch against him. She hovered on the edge of coming. When he brought the index finger of his other hand against her clit through the silk and pressed in and around just once, she couldn't hold back.

Her pussy convulsed and released more moisture. She pressed her swollen lips against his palm, too sensitive to continue thrusting, but enjoying his touch too much to move away. Her breasts ached as her orgasm peaked, and the convulsions faded to tiny spasms.

He was the first to break contact. Demi removed his hands and stood up to his full height. Gently, he drew her up to stand with him and pulled her close for a tender kiss. When he lifted his head, he caressed her cheek. "Did you enjoy that, *meu dragostia*?"

She leaned against him. "I nearly died," she said against his chest.

He laughed, and it caused his chest to rumble. "I should leave you to rest."

She shook her head, grinning when the light dusting of hair on his chest tickled her cheeks. "Not yet."

"You want to continue?"

"Yes." She bit back a yawn as a wave of tiredness swept through her. "I've never felt anything like that." She lifted her head to meet his eyes. "I've had orgasms before, but never like that. I feel like I'm just getting started." She was unable to block the yawn that followed her words.

Demi kissed her forehead. "But you're near collapsing, Anca. There will be another chance for lovemaking. The first time should be slow and sensual, not hindered by your exhaustion."

Her eyes darted to the hard bulge in his pants. "What about you?"

He shrugged. "I'll survive a bit of discomfort."

Anca licked her lips. "You don't have to."

He shook his head. "You're too exhausted. I can't allow you to tire yourself any further."

She took his hand and walked to the bed on shaking legs. He followed behind her without a word. When she let go of his hand, he stood in front of her with his eyebrow quirked, staring at her. His eyes widened as she pushed off her pants and panties. "Your pussy is smooth."

She nodded. "I like to swim, and I don't like hair showing. It's just as easy to have it all waxed."

Demi's brows furrowed. "Is this a common practice in America?"

Anca shrugged. "It depends on the woman."

His eyes remained on her pussy. He reached out and stroked it hesitantly. "I have never seen a woman with a bald pussy before. I have heard of it, and I have always been curious to touch one…to taste a smooth pussy."

She felt a twinge of jealousy at the mention of other women. Anca kept her expression bland to keep from revealing her emotions. "Do you like it? Is it what you expected?"

"More." Demi stroked her smooth lips once more before dropping his hand to his side. "I like it very much. It makes my cock so hard it hurts."

Anca winked at him. "Good." She sat down on the bed and sank a few inches into its soft depths. She was nearly eye-level with his cock, so close she could see it twitching against the confines of his pants. "We both know you'll take care of it yourself as soon as you leave me."

Demi nodded, without a hint of embarrassment. "Yes."

Anca patted the soft coverlet. "I don't want you to leave me. I don't want to sleep alone tonight, in a strange place."

He frowned. "You want me to stay with you tonight?"

She nodded. "I might be afraid otherwise." She grinned up at him.

"There are guards—"

She sighed at his thick-headedness, unable to decide if it was deliberate. "Okay, forget subtlety. I want to feel your arms around me."

He blinked, and then nodded. "If that's what you want."

"I want more than that, but I'm too tired." She smiled again. "However, I'm not too tired to watch you please yourself."

A hint of uncertainty appeared in his eyes. "Anca?"

"I want to watch you stroke your cock." She shrugged. "I've always been aroused by a man pleasing himself. If I want to watch you, and if you aren't shy, there's no reason to be uncomfortable."

Demi tilted his head. "I don't know…"

She leaned forward to unzip his pants. He didn't push her hands away, so Anca pushed them down to his knees and stroked his cock through his sensible white briefs. It jumped against her hand, and she could feel it throbbing. "Please, Demi."

When he remained silent, she looked up at him through the veil of her lashes. His expression bordered on pain. When she trailed her nails against the head, he drew in a ragged breath. She grew bolder by his continued silence and slipped his cock from his briefs.

He stood there as rigid as a statue, while his cock jutted toward her, begging for her touch. Anca leaned forward a little more and kissed the head. His fluid smeared across her lips, and she looked up to ensure he was watching. She flicked out her tongue and swirled it around her lips slowly.

He swallowed audibly, and his cock seemed to harden in her hand. Anca reached for his hand and brought it to his cock. He cupped it without her urging.

"What do you feel?" she asked, repeating his earlier question.

Sweat beaded his upper lip, and he cleared his throat. "Smooth skin, hard, aching…" He trailed off and began stroking his cock.

Anca's sated body stirred with arousal again as she watched his hand engulfing the length of his cock. Her lips parted when he paused to softly stroke the V where all the nerve endings met.

Her eyes moved up to his face, and she smiled at his expression. His eyes were closed, his head was tossed back, and he was biting his lip. She returned her gaze to his stroking hand and, as he increased the tempo, her pussy spasmed.

He moaned low in his throat and squeezed his hand around the base of his cock. After a long second, he stroked upward again, moving slowly. His thumb caressed the corona of his cock, and he arched his hips.

Anca could see the way his muscles tightened, and she knew he was close. As he tightened his grasp and stroked downward, she cupped his balls in her hand. While she stroked them, she leaned forward and put her mouth around the head of his cock. Hot spurts of fluid filled her mouth, and she swallowed them as she continued caressing his balls.

Demi had stiffened when she put her mouth on him, but now he surged forward. He buried his other hand in her hair to hold her against him as he squeezed the last drop of arousal from his cock.

His cock softened in her mouth, and Anca eased away once he loosened his grip on her hair. She propped her chin against his hard stomach and stared up at him. It should have felt awkward, or maybe even embarrassing, but all she felt was a surge of tenderness that he had shared something so personal with her.

Her pussy ached with desire, but she was too tired. Anca caressed his buttocks with her hand, waiting for him to speak. He didn't seem inclined to break the silence, so she said, "I know what I'll be dreaming about tonight."

He lifted a brow. "What?"

"Making love to you." She yawned. "I'm ready for you, but I can't seem to keep my eyes open. I'm too tired to even take a bath."

Demi moved away from her. After he shed his pants, briefs, and shoes, he walked to the water pitcher and basin on the vanity table. She heard water splashing as he cleaned himself, and when he returned, he held a wet cloth. "Lie back."

Tears misted Anca's eyes as she lay back against the feather pillows and parted her legs. Never had any man been so tender with her or put so much emphasis on her needs. Until she met Demi, she hadn't thought such men existed, outside of fairy tales and romance books.

When he finished, he took the cloth into the bathroom before returning to her.

Anca managed to roll over so he could pull down the covers on her side of the bed. After he did so, she snuggled under them and buried her head in the pile of pillows. She was vaguely aware of Demi turning off the lamp before he got in bed with her. Almost as soon as he took her in his arms, her eyes closed, and she fell into a deep sleep.

* * * * *

When Anca's eyes opened later in the night, the travel alarm she'd unpacked and placed on the nightstand read 3:06 a.m. She had set it to Corsovan time before dinner, so she subtracted seven hours to get New York time. It was eight at night to her body, so it was little wonder she was awake and refreshed.

The time difference wasn't the only thing causing her to be alert, she realized. The blankets had been pushed aside, and there was a chill in the air. She noticed that right before she realized Demi's mouth was at her neck, sucking softly on her skin. His fingers were stroking her pussy.

She tilted her head to look at him, but his face at her neck kept her from moving far. "Demi?" Her voice still held traces of sleep.

He moved his mouth away from her neck slightly. "I couldn't sleep with you curled so temptingly in my arms. I'm sorry if I woke you."

"It's okay," she said in a dreamy voice, parting her legs so he could reach her clit more easily. He fumbled a moment before finding it, and then his thumb and forefinger were tracing light circles around the nub. She sighed and started to turn onto her back, but he stopped her by putting his mouth against her throat again.

Anca focused her gaze on a tapestry on the gray stone wall as Demi caressed her clit and sucked on her neck. She locked her thighs around his arm as he slid a finger inside her pussy. She circled her hips as she moaned.

Demi's other arm was pinned under her waist, but he repositioned her slightly so he could stroke her nipples. "I want to make love to you. Will you accept me?"

She stifled the urge to giggle at his formal request. Most men would have assumed they could proceed if they had their hands between their partner's thighs. She swallowed to suppress the laughter. "Yes."

She heard him move away from the bed. When he came into her line of sight, she watched him pad across the floor to lift his pants. He rummaged through the pockets until he found what he sought. She turned her head to watch him come back to the bed, and she saw he held a condom. He moved behind her, and she heard him opening the wrapper seconds before the bed dipped under his weight.

To her surprise, Demi didn't turn her onto her back, and he made no move to straddle her once he was back in bed. Instead, he stretched out behind her and lifted her thigh with his hand. He shifted her gently until she was angled with her head barely on the pillows, and her feet pointing toward the opposite corner of the bed.

Anca shivered as Demi positioned his leg across her thighs. His other leg pushed under hers to lift it. He nudged the leg he held a little higher in the air. His cock brushed against her buttocks as he scooted forward another inch. She bit her lip as she waited for him. Within seconds, the head of his cock was pushing against the wet entrance of her pussy.

He eased into her with a slow thrust, moving so slowly she thought she might pass out. A twinge of discomfort accompanied his total possession, and she stiffened. She immediately forced herself to relax.

Demi stopped moving. He cleared his throat. "You are a...virgin, Anca?"

She shook her head. "No. It's just been a long time."

"I see." He sounded disappointed. "Do you wish to continue?"

"Oh, yes. It didn't really hurt. I was just surprised..." She trailed off with a sigh. "I do want you."

He didn't speak as he withdrew carefully and thrust into her again. Each movement was slow and careful, as though he thought she was made of glass and might break.

It was disconcerting to be making love to him without seeing his expression. She could feel his body's reaction to her, and could hear his ragged breathing, but she couldn't see how he felt. She wanted to look into his eyes.

When he withdrew again, Anca pulled away from him. She pulled her legs away from his and rolled over onto her other side, so she was facing him. He was frowning.

"Is something wrong?"

She smoothed her fingers over his furrowed brow. "No. I wanted to see you...to look into your eyes as we make love." She moved closer to him, until her breasts touched his chest. Anca put her thigh over his legs, exposing her pussy.

Demi thrust forward, and his cock pushed against her clit. She scooted up a bit, and he entered her pussy again. Once inside her, he stopped moving, and their eyes locked.

Anca stared into his dark eyes, and a sensation of rightness swept through her. The physical presence of his body joined with hers wasn't as intense as the emotions flashing through his eyes, transmitting themselves to her. She felt loneliness sweep over her, followed by longing. His eyes reflected the image of her face, and when she saw herself in them, contentment washed over her.

She felt connected to Demi on a level she had never experienced with another man. As he moved away from her, and then surged back inside her with a powerful thrust, her heart raced. Perspiration formed on her brow, and she struggled to get closer to him.

"What do you see in my eyes?" Demi asked, as he draped his arm over her waist and squeezed her buttocks.

Anca struggled to focus on his question as he rocked his hips, while pressing her closer still. He filled her completely when his cock pushed into her pussy. Her eyes were starting to water, but she didn't want to blink and risk missing the play of emotions in his eyes. "Uh…"

He thrust into her more forcefully. "You wanted to look. Tell me what you see."

"You. Me." She couldn't think, couldn't breathe. How was she supposed to answer his question when she couldn't concentrate on anything but the whirling vortex of his eyes and the way they fit together perfectly?

Demi released her bottom and trailed his hand over her hip, across her belly, and down to her pussy. He slipped his fingers between her smooth lips and circled her clit with small strokes. "Do you know what I see in your eyes?"

"Uh…" she said again, unable to form coherent thoughts.

"Pleasure, confusion, longing. More than that…"

She closed her eyes as the sensations overwhelmed her. He thrust into her again and continued caressing her clit in time with each tilt of their hips.

"Open your eyes," he said forcefully. His voice had previously been a rough whisper.

Anca's eyes popped open, and she looked up at him, barely able to focus on his face, because she was so close to coming.

"You wanted to watch me while we made love." He pushed his cock deep inside her and stopped moving. "Tell me."

There was a strange sense of desperation about him, as though he *needed* her answer. She blinked, struggling to speak as he resumed moving inside her. She swallowed and forced her eyes open and into focus as her gaze locked with his.

Previously, she had let the emotions blur together, but now she tried to separate them. Tenderness, that was easy to spot. Pleasure, of course. His eyes were expressive, but more than that, she seemed to know what he was feeling as he felt it.

Were the emotions really in his eyes, or was she sensing them directly from him? The experience was similar to a vision, but different too. The emotions were more specific, and less open to interpretation. Rather than *seeing*, she was *feeling*. Or was she? Was it all in her mind?

"Anca?" His eyes pleaded with her as his muscles quivered. "Now, please, tell me if you can see what I'm feeling. I can't wait..."

Her orgasm swept over her as his body stiffened and his cock spasmed. Anca put her hand on his shoulder and dug her nails into his skin. The answer suddenly crystallized in her mind, and she wondered why she hadn't realized earlier. It seemed so obvious. "Love," she forced out through gritted teeth as convulsions swept through her body.

Demi sagged against her, and his relief was palpable. "Yes," he whispered against her neck. His lips tickled her skin. He whispered something, but the words were indistinct. It sounded like he said, "Joined," but she couldn't be certain.

Tiredness swept over Anca as the pleasure from her orgasm slowly faded away. A feeling of being protected accompanied the languorous afterglow of making love, and she curled closer to Demi. Questions flickered through her mind, but she didn't voice them. She was too tired to talk...if only she was too tired to think.

She should ask why Demi thought he loved her. She should tell him their lovemaking didn't change anything. She was still returning home at the end of the week. She should make it clear what they had done tonight was a mistake and wouldn't—couldn't—happen again.

The only problem was, it didn't feel like a mistake. For the first time in her life, Anca wasn't haunted by the ever-present, phantom sensation that something was missing. Sex had never filled that ache before, so why did it now?

She didn't want to examine it too closely, because a shadowy answer had already formed in her mind. Being with Demi had been more than sex, but she refused to allow herself to define exactly what else it had been. Such thoughts would be dangerous to her future, and they threatened to upset the life she was accustomed to.

His arm draped her waist again, and he turned his head so his mouth was against her ear. "I have to leave you soon."

Her sleep-heavy eyelids had started to close, but she opened them quickly. "What? Why?" She frowned. "Is it illegal or something to make love if you aren't married?"

He laughed, and his chest rumbled against hers. "No, though it would probably be better not to have rumors circulating about your sex life during your first week here." He eased away and propped his chin on his hand. "I have a duty to perform, and I must leave around daybreak."

"Where are you going?"

"Ylenia is staying at Necheau, a village high in the mountains. Her niece married into the pa...one of the groups who live there. She left to visit her weeks ago, before your father sent me to find you." His lips curved into a small smile. "Though I doubt she didn't know he would send for you. Little escapes Ylenia."

The name was familiar. "Who's Ylenia again?"

"She's our spiritual leader, and she will want to meet you immediately." His expression darkened. "She will have much to tell you, and not all of it will be pleasant."

A hint of foreboding overshadowed the contentment of lying in his arms. Anca wasn't anxious to meet this woman. A shiver raced down her spine, and she bit back the urge to beg him not to fetch the woman. She sensed the meeting was unavoidable, though she didn't know how she knew that.

"When will you be back?" She tried to force herself to sound cheery, to hide her reluctance to meet Ylenia, and her reluctance to be parted from him. Unfortunately, her voice emerged more as a croaky chirp.

"Late tonight or early tomorrow. I'll take a Land Rover to get into the mountains, but Ylenia will insist on returning on horseback. She gets violently carsick."

"What will I do with myself?"

"You are free to do anything you wish." He touched her cheek and smoothed his fingers over her supple skin. "Don't go anywhere alone though. It may not be safe." He seemed reluctant to divulge that last bit of information. "Take Starr. She has agreed to be your companion while you're here."

Anca's brow quirked. "She *agreed*? How does one get a wolf to agree to anything?"

He seemed to be going out of his way to be obtuse. "Carefully, and with much persuasion." He grinned at her.

"But—"

"You will be safe with her."

She shivered, imagining having the wolf shadowing her every move. She would rather take her chances alone.

"Anca, promise me something." He spoke in a low voice, and his expression was somber.

"What?"

"Promise me you won't try to leave while I'm gone. I know you're frightened of what everyone expects from you, but please promise me you'll be here when I get back."

She frowned when she realized the thought of leaving while he wasn't there to stop her hadn't even entered her mind. "I'll stay until the end of the week, as I agreed to."

He nodded, not looking satisfied, but no longer looking fearful. "I'll return soon." He cupped her face in his hand. "I find the thought of leaving you painful, now that we have joined."

"I'll miss you," she said again and snuggled closer to him. A hint of worry lingered as he pulled the blankets over them and relaxed. Even as his soft snores filled the chamber a few minutes later, she remained on edge. She didn't know which she dreaded more—being alone in the castle for the day with a wolf companion; meeting Ylenia and hearing what she had to say; or telling Demi she had to go back to her real life.

An ache near her heart caused her to catch her breath, and it answered her question. What she dreaded most was leaving Demi, though she wasn't certain how such a turn of events had happened so quickly. All she knew was she wanted to be with him, though they had known each other only a few days. It felt like she had always known him, and she had simply been waiting for him.

Yet, how could she stay? She wasn't meant to be a queen, even if she had wanted that kind of life. She'd had no training, breeding, or warning about her expected role in Corsova.

He would just have to understand she couldn't stay here. Even if she refused to take over for her father, people would always expect her to change her mind if she didn't return to New York. It would be worse to live in the country as a regular citizen, and she couldn't expect Demi to return home with her to New York. In her heart, she knew he couldn't easily leave his life in Corsova.

Anca would have to make him understand all that if he protested. It wouldn't be that difficult, once she got her stubborn heart to accept there wasn't any other way. Right now, that was the most daunting task facing her.

# Chapter Eight

The next time Anca awoke, she was alone, as expected. She sat up and turned her face in the direction of the large window. Sunlight flooded the room, and what she could see of the sky appeared blue and cloudless. She glanced at the clock on the nightstand and noted it was a little past ten a.m.

There was a knock at the door, and she wondered if that's what had awakened her. "Just a sec," she called as she slid from the bed and searched for her clothes. Demi had folded them neatly on the trunk at the foot of the bed. Anca slipped on the sweater as she padded to the door.

She opened it a crack and peeked out. Her brow furrowed when she saw Nikia standing in the doorway. "Er, good morning." She ran her hands through her hair, hoping to hide some of the ravages caused by a night of lovemaking.

"Hello, sleepy head," Nikia chirped. She wore emerald-green jodhpurs and a white blouse. She clutched a wicked-looking crop in her right hand. "I thought you might like to join me in a ride."

Anca's first instinct was to refuse, but she stilled the impulse. If her sister was making an effort to welcome her, she should reciprocate by accepting. "That sounds nice, but I've only awakened—"

"I figured as much. I rapped on your door for several minutes." Her eyes gleamed with a hint of malice before she blinked. "Long night?"

"I didn't get much sleep." She strove for a cool tone as she met Nikia's eyes.

"Hmm." Nikia glanced at her wrist, examining her gold watch. "Why don't you shower and dress? I'll nip down to the kitchen for a light lunch to bring along. Will an hour be long enough?"

"Yes. Thank you for the invitation."

Nikia shrugged and turned to walk down the hall. "Meet me in Papa's study."

Anca watched her go for a few seconds, wondering if she shouldn't call the other woman back and rescind her acceptance. She sighed and shut the door, figuring it would please her father if she bonded with her sister. Perhaps her poor impression of Nikia from last night wasn't accurate. Maybe her sister had been as surprised by Anca's existence as she had been to discover she had a half-sister.

\* \* \* \* \*

Less than an hour later, Anca met Nikia in the study, after losing her way twice. She had wandered into a room full of tapestries she could have spent hours exploring, if not for Nikia waiting for her. As soon as she had the chance, she would return to that room — assuming she could find it again.

Nikia sat behind Valdemeer's desk, with her feet propped on the desk. The supple leather of her knee-boots was as soft and smooth as the crop in her hands. A picnic basket was on the edge of the desk.

Anca smoothed her hair, bound in a ponytail, and tried to resist the urge to compare her quiet beauty to the exotic allure of her half-sister. Something about the other woman made her feel inadequate. She forced a smile, wishing her jeans and shirt looked half as elegant as Nikia's garb. "I guess I'm ready."

"Sensible gear," Nikia said as she scanned Anca from head to foot. Her eyes seemed to linger on Anca's breasts for a moment longer than was comfortable. She stood up, and the moment passed.

Anca jumped when Nikia slapped the riding crop against her leg. "I should warn you I've never been riding before."

"I'm not surprised." Nikia shook her head. "I've heard your childhood was…impoverished."

She stiffened at the comment. "We didn't live in a castle, but we managed just fine."

A simpering smile curved across Nikia's face as she lifted a basket from the desk. "Of course you did. Still, it's a pity you weren't here in Corsova, where you belonged." She licked her lips. "I would have welcomed the opportunity to know you."

"Er, thanks." Anca was at a loss as to answering her sister. She followed Nikia silently from the study and through a twisting maze of rooms and hallways. As they left the castle through an entrance around the back, she asked, "Did you know about me?"

"Of course. I was six when Katrine abandoned Papa."

She frowned at Nikia's stiff tone. "Were you and Mother close?"

Nikia shrugged, letting that be her answer. She shifted the basket to her other hand and tucked the crop under her arm as they rounded the castle.

Anca caught her breath as Nikia swung open a gate and they emerged into a meadow. The lush grass was a brilliant green, and conifers towered over them. As they walked past one, she couldn't resist touching the rough bark of the tree. "These trees must be ancient." The trunk was twice as wide as she was.

Nikia turned her head slightly. She sounded disinterested when she said, "Several hundred years old, in fact. Corsova has one of the largest areas of trees left from times when most forests were decimated to build buildings and create farmland. Wait until we ride into the mountains. Even larger trees are common, and the weald grows so thickly one could easily lose their way."

"How did these trees manage to avoid getting cut down?"

"Corsova has remained untouched by the outside world, for the most part. Even in the country's infancy, our people kept our borders sealed." She shrugged. "It is our way. We don't like outsiders."

Anca frowned as she caught a hint of warning in Nikia's voice. Was this outing just an opportunity for Nikia to warn her away from Corsova and her supposed rightful place as queen? She could save her breath, and Anca would tell her that if she brought up the subject. "I see."

Soon, they approached a building larger than Anca's entire block in New York. A clear stain preserved the natural beauty of the weathered wood. A faint scent of manure wafted through the air as they neared the two open wooden doors.

Before they even stepped inside, a young man came rushing out of the dim interior of the stables. He bowed at the waist to Nikia, and then bowed even lower—if that was possible—to Anca. "Your Highnesses," he said in a hushed tone.

"Emil, we wish to ride." Nikia seemed unaware of the innate haughtiness in her tone. "Saddle Brutus for me. Pigeon will do for Anca, since she has never ridden before."

He hurried to obey her commands.

Anca followed him into the stables, aware of Nikia trailing behind her. She looked down the aisle, trying to guess how many stalls the huge room held. She guessed at least fifteen on each side of the aisle, with those closest to her all occupied.

She stopped at the nearest stall and eyed the chestnut standing there. The horse's brown eyes seemed to be examining her with equal interest, before it tossed its head, sending its blond mane flowing around its head.

"Rachel," Nikia said. She clicked her tongue, and the mare pressed herself against the stall. She caressed Rachel's ears, and the horse whinnied. She turned her head in Anca's direction. "It is quite safe to touch her. She won't hurt you."

Anca was reluctant to reach out for the horse, though she didn't think Rachel would hurt her. The mare seemed placid, but she had no experience with equines. She held out her hand, but didn't quite touch the horse's neck.

Nikia made an impatient sound low in her throat and captured Anca's hand. She pressed it against the horse and forced Anca to stroke her. "See? She enjoys your touch."

"Uh…" Anca patted the horse feebly before she tried to disengage Nikia's hold. Her sister's grip tightened as she pressed her hand more firmly against Rachel's short coat. "She's softer than I expected."

"Rachel responds to affection—the soothing tone of voice, the confident stroke..." Nikia trailed off as she turned Anca's hand slightly to caress her palm. "The softness of your hand pleases her." Nikia's eyes gleamed, and she licked her lips. "Do you like caressing her?"

"She's very nice," Anca said inanely. She made an effort to tug away her hand again and was relieved when Nikia released it. She sagged with relief when Emil and another dark-haired boy—even younger than he—appeared, leading two horses.

It was obvious at first glance which horse was Nikia's. Brutus stood straight and proud, with a seemingly instinctive superiority reflected in his stance. His eyes were almost as dark as his glossy coat, and his white mane contrasted beautifully.

In comparison, Pigeon was rather pathetic-looking. The horse was sway-backed, and its mottled gray coat looked ragged in places. The horse barely lifted his head when Emil stopped before Anca. "Your horse, Highness."

"Thanks." She gave him a smile before turning apprehensive eyes to the old horse. Despite his serene attitude, she couldn't help a twinge of nerves. What did she, a city kid, know about dealing with horses?

Emil seemed to sense her unease, because he assisted her into the saddle. "Move with his gait," he said in heavily accented English. "Let Pigeon do the work and follow his lead. If he goes too fast or you get scared, pull on the reins and say, 'Whoa'. He will stop immediately." He appeared skeptical about the horse ever going too fast. "Lady Nikia is an accomplished horsewoman. She will assist you if you get in trouble."

His words failed to reassure her as she grasped the reins and clenched her legs around the horse. Nikia led the way, keeping Brutus at an easy canter. Anca struggled to relax and move with the horse. Once she remembered to keep her thighs clenched and her feet in the stirrups, she was able to loosen her death grip on the reins.

Soon, they were riding into a denser concentration of trees. Anca paused to look behind her and saw the stable was farther away than she would have guessed. It seemed the last few minutes had crawled by as she struggled to get a basic grasp of riding.

Nikia drew up on Brutus's reins and turned the horse slightly in her direction. "Is something wrong?"

Anca shook her head, unwilling to voice her continued anxiety. "Just fine," she said with a false smile.

"Excellent. Let's speed up a bit." Nikia kicked the horse to spur him into moving.

She swallowed thickly and kicked lightly against Pigeon's sides. The horse took off with a small jolt, and she tightened her hold on the reins. The horse seemed to be fine without her direction, and he increased his speed to match Brutus's.

Soon, she was riding near the flank of Nikia's horse. The light wind blew through her hair, making her glad she had restrained it. The steepness of the hill and the profusion of flowers distracted Anca from thoughts of her appearance. Purple, yellow, red, and pink blooms seemed to explode from the ground in huge clumps. There was no clear trail, and Pigeon's hooves trampled several of the blooms.

She was so intent on the scenery that it took her several minutes to realize the horses were nearly running.

As soon as she realized how fast they were moving, panic took over, and she pulled up so hard on the reins that Pigeon neighed in protest. He shuddered to a halt, and his withers trembled.

Anca took a deep breath, striving to calm her racing heart. Nikia continued to ride, seeming not to realize she had fallen so far behind. She was half-tempted to let her keep riding while she turned around and headed back to the stables, but she didn't. "Nikia," she shouted as she urged Pigeon into a slow canter.

Nikia halted and turned. She waited until Anca had caught up. She shook her head. "There's nothing to be frightened of."

Anca shrugged. "Sorry to fall behind."

"No matter." She slapped the crop against Brutus's flank, and he rushed forward with a neigh. Nikia's legs seemed securely clamped around the horse, and she didn't bat an eyelash when he reared in mid-air.

Anca shuddered at the sound the horse's hooves made as he hit the ground. She had a disconcerting image of being under those hooves. She closed her eyes, straining to discover if morbid imaginings prompted the mental-picture, or if she had caught a snatch of a vision. No further images came to her, and she opened her eyes.

It was difficult to keep up with the stride Nikia set, and Anca leaned over the horse and dug her knees into his sides. It was a jarring trip up the mountain, and even the blossoms and trees failed to hold her attention.

It seemed like hours had passed, and she was about to plead with Nikia to stop when her sister drew Brutus to a halt and turned partially in her saddle. She didn't look at all disheveled from their ride.

"We're near Bulgain Lake. I thought we would have lunch there and rest a bit before returning to the castle."

Anca nodded her agreement, too tired to verbalize one. She clung to Pigeon as they resumed the climb up the mountain, finding her resolve to hold on renewed by the promise of the ride ending soon. She decided not to think about the return ride down the mountain right then.

When they topped the rise, her breath caught in her throat. It was almost worth the ride just to see the lake. It stretched before them for at least a mile in each direction. Trees sheltered the shore of the sparkling blue water, and it was so clear it reflected the mountains nearby on its smooth surface.

A deer had been drinking from the lake, and it froze as they approached. Its nose twitched, and its body spasmed. Within seconds, it had broken its own paralysis and darted into the cover of the massive trees.

She pulled on Pigeon's reins, and he stopped without jarring her. Anca moved stiffly to dismount, wincing as her overworked muscles protested the sudden movement after two hours of remaining in an unaccustomed position.

Nikia hopped off Brutus in one smooth motion and looped his reins over a branch on a nearby tree. Anca led Pigeon forward to do the same thing, but Nikia shook her head. "He never runs away. Just let him wander a bit. He'll enjoy it." She patted Brutus's neck. "This is the one who craves freedom. You can't trust him not to run and never come back."

Anca followed her sister's suggestion of walking around to stretch her muscles while Nikia unpacked their lunch after spreading a white blanket she removed from the basket. Anca stopped near the edge of the lake and peered into the water. It appeared bottomless, and she wondered how deep it was. She knelt to plunge her cupped hands into the water and found it deliciously icy.

She splashed some on her flushed face and sighed at the coldness as it washed away the heat of the day and the morning's exertion. She heard a twig snap behind her and glanced up to see Nikia holding out a kerchief. Anca took it and dipped it in the lake. As she dabbed her cheeks and the back of her neck, she pointed to the clusters of pinkish-red blooms dotted around the edge of the lake. "What are those?"

"Rose bay. Some people call them carpet roses or common oleander."

Anca started as the name played through her mind. Abruptly, she remembered the vision of lying with Demi in moonlight, on a bed of rose bay. Her pussy clenched with arousal as she recalled the pleasure of making love with him. She hoped the vision was a prophecy and not a random flutter.

Once she had cooled off, Anca rose and walked with Nikia to the blanket. Whomever had packed the basket had included hard cheese, soft, crusty bread, a bottle of wine, and a flask of water. There were also two pears and two apples. She took the chunk of cheese and bread Nikia extended. To her surprise, Nikia didn't seem inclined to talk while they ate, so she concentrated on the light lunch. Remembering last night's experience with the wine, she stuck to water.

It was only after she returned the remains of their picnic to the basket that Nikia leaned back and eyed her with unnerving intensity. Anca folded her hands together and waited for her to begin. She had already guessed this outing was about more than the two of them becoming acquainted.

"Why did you come here?"

Anca twiddled her thumbs, but otherwise, she didn't betray her nervousness. "I wanted to meet my father before he died."

Nikia's brow furrowed. "Demi told you he was dying?"

She quirked a brow at the question. "Yes." Had he lied to trick her into coming with him?

She nodded. "It's closer than I thought," she muttered under her breath. "I didn't realize…" Nikia lifted her head, and her eyes were cold. "Do you think you can just come here and take over the throne, unchallenged?"

Anca shook her head, but she didn't get a chance to respond.

"It's mine! Do you hear me? I've waited all my life to be queen. You won't rob me of my place." Her cheeks were flushed with anger, and she was breathing heavily.

"I don't want to be a queen or a princess or any other nonsense this backward country offers me," Anca said coldly. "I have a life in New York, and I don't plan to give it up."

Nikia's eyes narrowed, and she studied her for several minutes. Finally, she nodded. "That's good. I won't surrender without a fight, you know."

Anca nodded, shivering at the threatening tone. She was abruptly aware of how alone they were and cursed her stupidity for attempting to bond with her sister. Her initial impression appeared to be the right one. She should have avoided Nikia's presence at all cost.

In a flash, Nikia's demeanor changed. "Well, now that's out of the way, are you ready to go back to the castle?"

Anca nodded, disconcerted by her sister's sunny disposition, so quickly following her angry outburst. "Yes. I've had enough riding today."

"Okay. Let's go." Nikia bounded to her feet and lifted the basket. She smiled. "I'm glad you came for a visit. I wanted to meet you."

"Er..." She floundered for a response, but Nikia didn't seem to notice. She followed more sedately as Nikia hurried to Brutus. Anca was several steps away when she saw the horse rear and knock her sister to the ground. She broke into a run, but by the time she reached Nikia, the horse was galloping away.

"Stupid horse," Nikia said angrily. She got to her feet before Anca could kneel beside her to check on her. "I'll have to catch him. Wait here for me."

"What?"

"I'll have to take Pigeon to see if I can catch up with him." She whistled to the gelding, and his ears perked. He trotted toward her. "If I don't, Brutus won't return to the stable, and the wolves might get him if he's out after dark."

"W-wolves?" she repeated in a shaky tone. "But—"

"Don't worry. It's daytime. I'll be back soon enough." Nikia clambered onto Pigeon. "If I don't try to catch Brutus soon, I won't be able to with Pigeon. I doubt he can keep pace."

"Why don't I come with you? We can ride double." As unappealing as that thought was, it was more attractive than the idea of staying alone by the lake, not knowing when Nikia would return.

Nikia laughed. "Carrying two riders, poor old Pigeon will never catch up with Brutus." She waved her arm. "I'll be back soon."

"Wait!"

Either Nikia didn't hear her, or she ignored the desperate shout. She rode off at a gallop, heading in the same direction Brutus had taken.

She was soon out of sight, leaving Anca alone. Despite the cloudless day and hot sun, a chill raced down her spine. She hugged herself and examined the area around the lake, looking for wolves and other creatures she had no wish to meet up with—not in daylight, and especially not in the dark.

\* \* \* \* \*

Anca stayed by the lake for several hours, though her fear didn't abate. She watched for Nikia's return, but the shadows cast by the sun on the trees shifted across the ground as the afternoon progressed, still without her sister's return.

She longed for her cell phone in its case, lying out in plain sight on a table in her room. Why hadn't she remembered to grab it? She scowled when she realized it would have been useless, even if she had it on her. She didn't know any Corsovan numbers, and 9-1-1 probably wasn't available here. At least she could have kept the boredom at bay by playing a few games.

As the time passed, she grew hungry. She tried ignoring it for a while, but her stomach started rumbling every few minutes. Not even her fear dampened her hunger, and she opened the picnic basket as the sun's strength started to fade. Anca found a partial loaf of bread and a wedge of cheese. The water flask was empty, and she eyed the wine warily, leaving it in the basket.

She nibbled on the cheese and bread, trying to make the small portions last. She had a brief thought of rationing them, since she had no idea how long it would be before someone found her. An even more disconcerting mental image of being eaten by wolves chased away that thought. She ate the provisions available to her, figuring she wouldn't last long enough to starve if she weren't rescued soon.

Her mouth was dry when she finished, and she cautiously uncorked the wine. She sniffed it and winced at the unpleasant copper smell. She wondered what type of grapes they grew in Corsova as she took a small sip.

Anca steeled herself for the same bittersweet taste as last night and was able to swallow without choking. She grimaced at the taste, but found it wasn't as unpleasant as the last glass she had tried. In fact, after a few minutes, she started enjoying the sharp tang and aftertaste it left in her mouth.

It had the peculiar effect of making her more hungry though, and she corked the bottle, knowing she had nothing else to eat right then. She didn't even have a passing knowledge of the flora of the Bulgain Mountains. Ripe, juicy berries beckoned from a bush nearby, but she didn't know if they were safe to eat. Though the purplish-blue fruit resembled blueberries, they could be poisonous.

As the sun slipped behind a group of clouds and the sky streaked with myriad colors, indicating sunset was near, Anca rose from the blanket she had spread out hours before. She walked around the perimeter of the lake a bit, searching for signs of anyone approaching.

"Hello?" she called out, cupping her hands around her mouth to make her voice carry. "Nikia?"

Her voice echoed back to her, followed by the cry of a bird, but no other sound reached her. She walked the opposite direction, near a thick growth of trees lining the crude path they had taken to the lake. She called out again, but there was no answer—not even the lonesome bird's cry.

She walked back to the clearing at the edge of the lake and examined the path. She remembered from riding that it was at least an hour's worth of riding back, but she didn't know what that would translate to if she walked it. Aside from that, she didn't know at what point to leave the trail or which direction to go. Nikia had led her on a twisting route from the castle, through trees, tall grass, and untamed land.

When they broke onto the path, she had asked why they hadn't taken it all the way. Nikia had explained it didn't lead back to the castle, but originated in the village of Grasov, which was in a different direction than Castle Draganescu.

Anca considered the path before she looked up at the sky. By the way the sun was so quickly waning, she knew she wouldn't make it back to the castle before nightfall. She probably wouldn't even make it to the point where she was supposed to leave the trail—if she could remember where that was. Since she had no idea how far away Grasov was, that didn't seem to be a viable option either.

With a disgruntled sigh, Anca dropped onto the blanket again and locked her arms around her knees. She rested her head on her thighs and cursed her stupidity for remaining at the lake for so long, waiting for Nikia to come back. If she had started walking hours ago, she probably would have been at the castle or the village by now.

She stiffened when she heard a wolf howl in the distance. She'd hoped Nikia had been toying with her when she mentioned wolves, but it appeared there were still some roaming Corsova.

Twilight would soon be upon her, and the dim sky already provided little illumination. Would fire repel the wolves or attract them? She wondered how difficult it would be to make a fire before she remembered she didn't have any matches. She hadn't even been a Girl Scout, so she didn't have a clue about creating a fire from striking stones or sticks, or whatever one struck.

All Anca could do was wait and hope someone came soon. Preferably, before she became dinner for a pack of wolves or other wild animals. Why hadn't she listened to her inner warnings and refused Nikia's invitation?

\* \* \* \* \*

"It's my fault." Starr's head was bowed, causing her light-brown hair to obscure her angular face. "I should have waited right by her door."

Demi sighed. "I told her to take you along if she left the castle. It's not your fault she didn't listen. Nikia had her part in whisking Anca away without an escort. Don't forget how manipulative she can be."

Starr shook her head. "It's my fault," she insisted. "I was derelict in my duties. If I've let Her Highness come to harm…"

Ylenia's soothing voice interrupted. "Assigning and accepting blame doesn't help right now. We must find Anca. She's out there alone."

"Worse," Demi said grimly. "She's with Nikia."

Starr made a soft sound of distress, but didn't repeat her statement about it being her fault. "I'll gather Sorin and Lucian to help me search. We'll go in wolf-form. We'll make better time that way."

"I'll come with you," Demi said. He began unbuttoning his shirt and averted his eyes as Starr slipped out of her robe. She quickly transformed and moved to Ylenia's side, pressing her furry body against the older woman's leg. He shed his clothes, but before transforming, he said to Ylenia, "Tell Valdemeer what's happened. Have him organize as many guards as he can, as quickly as possible. We have no idea which way Nikia led her, so we have a vast area to cover."

Ylenia nodded, and her wrinkled face clearly reflected her worry. "Shall I notify my niece and have her ask her leader to take his pack to search for her in their region?"

He hesitated, blanching at the idea of asking Rica for anything. "That's a long way from the castle. Would Nikia have led her so far?"

"Rica won't deny my request, if that's what you're thinking," she said in a soft voice. "He won't be happy to be called into the search, but he'll assist us."

With a small sigh, he laid aside his pride, knowing Anca's welfare was more important than honoring the pack's desire for isolation. "Very well." Demi found a small smile. "I wonder how Anca will react if we find her before the guards do."

He didn't wait for an answer as he closed his eyes and thought about transforming. He felt the familiar burning-stretching that accompanied the change. He looked down and saw his nose morph into a muzzle. Within seconds, he had transformed into a silvery-white wolf several inches taller and much more muscular than Starr. Side by side, they padded from the room. As she went to gather Sorin and Lucian, he broke into a loping run.

As soon as he exited the castle, he set off in the direction calling to him. He was almost certain he could feel Anca, and hoped his senses weren't deceiving him into going the wrong way. He broke into a run, without trying to pace himself. In his wolf-form, he couldn't access his mental powers as well, but he still knew she was in danger. He had to find her, and soon.

\* \* \* \* \*

The cry of a wolf, quickly followed by three other distinctive howls, sounded much too close for Anca's comfort. Full dark was upon the land, and she was questioning her decision to stay put. Yet, what alternative was there? She had already discarded the idea of walking down the path, at least until morning.

She eyed the towering trees, wondering if she could manage to shimmy up one for shelter. Could wolves climb trees? Surely not, since dogs couldn't...or could they? Oh, how she wished her mother had let her have a pet as a child.

Anca shivered as a brisk wind rustled through the trees. A while ago, she had gone from sitting on the tablecloth to huddling in it, but it was a meager wrap. She stood up and ran around in a circle, hoping exertion would raise her body temperature. Who would have expected the temperature to plummet from the mid-eighties during the day to the lower-forties at night?

She stiffened when she heard a furtive movement in the stand of trees nearby. Anca's eyes darted around the lake, but she couldn't make out much, even with the half-moon. She knelt down to pluck a sturdy branch from the ground where she had placed it earlier. It had been the best makeshift weapon she could find at the time.

She cast off the blanket and took what she hoped was an aggressive stance. She crouched slightly and spread her legs wider. She gripped the rough branch like a club and waited to see if the sound was in her imagination. Please let it be her imagination.

The rustling came again, this time closer, and accompanied by a low growl. Seconds later, a medium-sized wolf appeared in front of her.

Anca struggled to breathe as she told herself it was just a large dog from the village or the castle. The trio of howls that sounded from nearby didn't reinforce her supposition. She tightened her hands on the branch until her fingertips were numb and waited to see what the wolf would do. She prayed it was a lone wolf, but from the howls she'd heard, she assumed it was part of a pack.

The wolf walked forward boldly, with its tail swishing as enthusiastically as one of its domesticated cousins. Its eyes gleamed red in the moonlight, and there appeared to be a tinge of cinnamon-red to its thick coat. Saliva glistened on its muzzle, and as it stopped less than two feet away, there was no mistaking it was definitely a wolf, not a dog.

She whimpered low in her throat as the wolf bared its teeth in a growl. Anca shook her head, wondering if she had imagined the eager, almost playful, tone to its growl. Somehow, she doubted it was a game she would enjoy if the wolf were playing.

It moved so quickly she barely had time to swing the branch. One second, it stood in front of her, and the next, it had sprung into the air. Anca saw it speeding toward her face, and she brought up the branch.

*Too slow. Not enough force*, she thought to herself as the branch connected with a thwacking sound against the wolf's front paw. It howled with pain, but it barely slowed its assault. Anca tried to brace herself as the animal crashed into her and sent her sprawling.

The reality of being confronted by a set of deadly fangs was worse than anything she had imagined during the time she had waited for someone to lead her back to Castle Draganescu. The wolf was inches from her face, and Anca strained to hold it back or push it away.

It snapped at her, and its warm breath washed over her. Anca was disconcerted that the wolf's breath smelled of mint. Shouldn't it reek of death and blood?

She pushed aside the frivolous thought and concentrated on trying to hold off the wolf. She cried out as it surged forward. Before she could roll away or push it off, the wolf's fangs sank into her shoulder.

With a low growl, the wolf tore through the meaty part of her shoulder. Anca screamed with agony as the ragged edges of the wound rubbed together when the wolf withdrew.

She knew it hadn't finished its attack. She blinked back a wave of blackness descending over her eyes and tried to second-guess the wolf. It had gone for her neck, but missed — she had no doubt about that. It would surely try again. Why was it hesitating?

As she racked her brain for a way to fight the wolf, as she continued to push against its body with all her strength, she heard a dreaded sound: Vicious growls surrounded her. She glanced briefly over the shoulder of the wolf pinning her to the ground and couldn't hold back a small scream.

Four wolves ringed them in a half-circle. One of the wolves — the one with the darkest coat — was massive, with wide shoulders, deadly looking fangs, and a menacing growl that caused her stomach to heave with nausea. The others seemed almost insignificant, but she didn't fail to notice the light-brown one or the dark-brown one.

Anca froze when her gaze slid over the silvery-white wolf. There was something...familiar...about its eyes. She frowned, temporarily forgetting a wolf lay on her, intent on tearing out her throat. She couldn't seem to wrench her gaze from the silver wolf.

A whimper from the wolf pressing her into the ground caught Anca's attention, and she couldn't believe she had forgotten about her circumstances. She stood no chance against a pack of wolves, and with her blood flowing, surely they were stirred into a frenzy.

Yet, there was an eerie calm about the four wolves standing nearby. Each of their eyes was on the wolf pinning her down. Anca couldn't believe it when that wolf backed away, with its tail tucked between its legs. To her further shock, each of the wolves turned to face the wolf as it backed away, instead of focusing on Anca.

In what looked like a command, the silver wolf looked at the dark-brown wolf and jerked its head in the direction of the reddish wolf. Without so much as a glance her way, the dark-brown one broke into a run. The reddish wolf seemed to realize it was in danger, because it turned and raced across the clearing, plunging into the forest with little regard for stealth. The dark-brown wolf remained in pursuit.

Anca eased into a sitting position, wondering if she could get up a tree before the wolves remembered she was there. Her heart dropped into her stomach as the silver wolf turned to eye her again. Its gaze was intent as it studied her, and then turned to the light-brown wolf. When it made a low sound, the light-brown wolf loped down the trail.

She bit back a scream as the massive wolf and the silver wolf approached her. It took her a moment to realize their posture was almost submissive, and they didn't seem to have the same aura of menace as the first wolf that attacked her. She was almost unsurprised when the silver wolf hunkered down on its belly and slithered toward her.

She still withdrew her feet, pressing her knees into her stomach, when the silver wolf sniffed her tennis shoe. She whimpered as the dark wolf plopped down beside her, though not near enough to touch her. Only the silver wolf seemed so bold as to initiate contact. He laid his head on her knee and whined softly.

It felt like someone else controlled her hand as she lifted it to stroke the wolf's silky fur. He tilted his head in the direction of her hand, pressing his ears more firmly against her fingers.

The explanation suddenly presented itself. Her father must make a practice of keeping tamed wolves as pets.

Apparently, these wolves had been part of the effort to find her. She briefly wondered how they had recognized her, but assumed the process worked the same as one for bloodhounds used by police and rescue services. The wolves must have smelled something containing her scent.

She felt a glimmer of fear as the wolf pressed itself closer to her body and sniffed her wound. Anca stiffened when its tongue flashed across the gaping wound. She jerked away and had the disconcerting sensation the wolf was reprimanding her with his steady gaze.

She covered the wound with her hand to hide it from the wolf. Domesticated or not, she thought blood might be too much temptation for a wolf, and she did not intend to be dinner for this one, after narrowly escaping that fate with the first one.

As the minutes passed, Anca's eyes grew heavier. She experienced an odd floating sensation, and didn't know if it was from blood loss or something else. A strange thought flickered across her mind—that she was sharing her body with another presence. This presence wasn't intrusive, but it was tuned into her thoughts, fears, and feelings through a tenuous link.

She tried fighting the urge to sleep, not fully trusting her wolf companions, but she was unable to keep her eyes open. A wave of exhaustion swept through her, and she found herself lying on her back with no memory of stretching out. She yawned and looked over at the silvery wolf as it nestled close to her, providing warmth and comfort. The massive wolf curved itself against her back, further warming her. Despite her best efforts to resist, she was soon asleep.

# Chapter Nine

Anca was aware of the cool touch of a cloth on her brow and the soothing whispers from a woman near her ear. She opened her eyes, but all she saw was a swirl of bright colors that didn't form a cohesive pattern. Her breathing was raspy, and tremors shook her body. Her shoulder felt like it was on fire, and the sensation was spreading down her arm and into her chest.

"Easy," came Demi's voice, followed by the touch of his hand on her brow. "Remain calm, *meu dragostia*. Let Ylenia work."

She whimpered with fear, unable to summon the ability to speak. She felt...strange. Her head was as light as it would have been if filled with helium. The fire from her wound continued to spread, alternating between burning-hot and icy-cold.

"Drink this," said a raspy feminine voice in thickly accented English.

She felt the edge of a cup placed against her lips, and she parted them. A noxious-tasting brew filled her mouth, and she choked.

"Swallow it," the woman insisted. "You must rest."

Anca managed a few sips, but her stomach churned with nausea, making her afraid to attempt to drink more. She managed a feeble wave, and someone withdrew the cup. A fog as thick as molasses descended on her, and the light-headed sensation changed to one of heaviness. Her body grew numb, blocking out the pain from the wound, and her eyelids closed.

"Is she asleep?" Demi asked.

She heard the same woman answer, though the words sounded distorted. "It's more like a twilight state, Nicodemus."

"Will it stop the change?"

Anca's brow furrowed, and she parted her lips to speak. She found her mouth too numb to form words.

"I don't know. I've never tried to prevent the process before. Always, our kind has chosen to consume the blood of the pack."

There was a note of distress in Demi's voice. "You have to do something to stop it. She didn't get a chance to decide. Already, so much will be thrust upon her…"

"Easy," the woman said soothingly. "I'll do my best, but I don't know how to stop it. I've never heard of anyone successfully interrupting a transformation."

"It isn't fair to Anca."

She wanted to ask what wasn't fair, but she still couldn't speak. Their conversation flowed around her, with some words making sense, while others seemed foreign. She didn't know if they slipped back and forth between Corsovan and English, or if she just couldn't follow.

"Most of our people choose to have the ability to transform. Surely, she would have done so. It is not so bad—"

Demi made a low sound. "We'll see how bad it is later tonight, if she transforms and lives." His tone turned arctic. "Nikia should die for what she's done today."

His harsh tone of voice and even harsher words sharpened Anca's attention.

The woman sighed. "Valdemeer will not do that."

"Then I will!" Demi snarled forcefully.

"You would not harm her, no matter what she did. Your soul is too gentle."

Anca tried to force her eyes open and keep her mind on their words, sensing the conversation was really happening, and wasn't just a product of her fevered mind. It seemed important for her to hear every word.

"This is my lifemate, Ylenia. She could have died. She will most certainly receive the ability to transform to wolf-form, and that could kill her the first time. My soul may be gentle," he said scathingly, "but I'm feeling anything but gentle right now."

"I do understand," Ylenia said softly, "but now, let your thoughts be on Anca and helping her, not consumed with vengeance."

"How do I help her?"

Anca appreciated his unhesitating offer, and she tried to thank him. Again, she found her mouth frozen.

"Your blood will help the wound heal."

"How? She hasn't lived as one of us—"

"Her body will know what to do," Ylenia interrupted. "She isn't generations removed from our way of life. She will easily adapt to our ways, when the time comes."

Anca felt someone lifting her into a semi-sitting position, and her head spun. Bile rushed up her throat, and whoever supported her must have realized she was about to vomit, because they pressed her face into a ceramic chamber pot seconds before she lost the contents of her stomach.

She managed to make a small sound of distress when she was eased away from the pot, but still held in a sitting position. Could the bite of a wolf have done so much damage? Was she in a hospital? Did they have hospitals in Corsova?

The questions flew from her mind when someone pressed their palm to her mouth. She recognized Demi's scent from spending the night with him. The edges of her mouth turned down in a feeble frown when she felt something warm and sticky flow onto her lips.

"Drink," he said. His hand didn't move.

As Anca's tongue slipped through her teeth, she tried to draw it back in. He didn't really want her to drink blood, did he? His blood, specifically. What kind of quackery did the doctors here use? She tried to protest, but instead, licked the blood from his wound.

She craved more. Instinct seemed to take over, and she was soon sucking from his hand, drawing in the blood as fast as it flowed, making impatient sounds when it slowed to a trickle.

"That's enough," Ylenia said.

Anca whimpered when he withdrew his hand and eased her back onto the bed. Once again, lethargy swept through her, and she struggled against her eyelids' compulsion to close. She wanted to demand answers for what was happening to her, but was too weak. Even now, she wondered how she had found the strength to do what they had asked.

*To drink his blood*, a tiny voice whispered in the back of her mind. Rather than repulse her, the thought caused her to tremble with excitement, and she longed for more. It was a blessing when her eyes closed, and she was able to escape the reality of enjoying consuming his blood.

\* \* \* \* \*

Demi paced to the window and gazed up at the moon before turning and making another circuit around Anca's bed. He paused briefly to touch her leg, and he winced at the heat. Something more intense than a fever ravaged her body, and he felt helpless, knowing he could do nothing to help her.

Ylenia had gone to bed to snatch a few hours of sleep, leaving Demi to monitor her. He had wanted to protest her leaving, but he knew if Ylenia couldn't stop the transformation, she couldn't help Anca if her body tried to reject the process. He could only hope his lifemate was strong enough to endure the change.

If someone survived the first transformation after a bite from a werewolf, his or her body was able to handle the change. If Anca had been raised in the old ways, he would have had little fear of her not surviving her first transformation.

However, since she had lived as a human all her life, he knew she was more vulnerable and in greater risk of dying. Humans were frail, and half of them were incapable of withstanding the change. Since she was weakened by Nikia's bite that hadn't fully healed, her body was more likely to reject the transformation and cause her to die.

His hands balled into fists as he imagined the pleasure of fastening his hands around Nikia's throat. He was glad of the guards keeping her locked in her room, for they kept him out. At that moment, he could imagine no greater pleasure than killing her, but he fought the urge. He refused to betray his king, and to violate Valdemeer's orders not to harm Nikia would be to turn his back on Valdemeer, Corsova, and his role in its future.

How could the old man be so blind?

He tried to squash the disloyal thought, knowing Valdemeer's conflicting emotions of guilt and hatred for his daughter made it impossible for him to deal with her without bias.

His attention turned from thoughts of Nikia to Anca as a thin wail issued from her. She had kicked off the blankets, and a sheen of sweat covered her nude body. He couldn't help a twinge of arousal at the sight of her beauty, but he didn't allow it to interfere with tending to her.

He knelt by the bed and touched her forehead. Her skin burned to the touch. As he stroked her cheek, he felt fur bristling through her skin. The transformation had begun. She made another sound low in her throat, and it emerged as an aborted howl.

He held her hand as dark-brown fur grew over her body. When her hand began to take the shape of a paw, he moved away and shed his own clothes. He waited until she was screaming and writhing with pain, as she became a medium-sized wolf, before he approached the bed again.

She was breathing heavily, and her tongue lolled out of her mouth, but her brown eyes were alert and questioning. He kept eye contact as he transformed to wolf-form. He saw her pupils dilate with shock. She shook her head, and then froze, seeming to realize she wasn't in human-form.

*It's okay*, he said to her, using his mind. He wondered if she would be able to communicate with him at all, since her mental powers were stunted from years of living as a human.

She blinked, and her eyes narrowed, but she didn't respond.

*Come with me.*

After a brief hesitation, she got on all fours and stepped down carefully from the bed. She shook, and her fur rustled. She cocked her head to examine her body.

*You'll adjust to the form soon. In fact, it can be quite liberating to run full-tilt through the forest without any concern, except catching your next meal.* He felt a glimmer of a thought come from her, but she couldn't make it take form. *Concentrate on what you want to tell me. My blood flows through your veins, giving you the strength to communicate. More than that, we have joined. You can speak to me more easily than you can to any other. It will happen naturally, if you let it.*

Her gaze locked with his, and she seemed to be concentrating. After several seconds, the thoughts became clear.

*What's happening?*

*Nikia's bite changed you.*

*Changed? How?*

*Corsova is a haven for many who would not fit in with humans. One of the bonds our people have formed over the centuries is with werewolves. Our blood gives them prolonged life, and consuming their blood just once allows us to transform into a wolf for the rest of our lives. Most of our people undergo the ritual in their early teens, as our bodies are more adaptable then.*

Her tail drooped, and her ears dropped flat against her skull. Her eyes appeared glazed, and she seemed to be having difficulty absorbing what he was telling her. The question she asked next surprised him. *I thought there had to be a full moon.*

She was definitely overwhelmed, he decided, to ask about something so inconsequential at that moment.

*Let's walk,* he suggested. Once she fell in step beside him, he attempted to explain the transformation. *Changing into a wolf isn't dependent on the time of the month or phase of the moon. As you gain control of the ability, you'll be able to transform at will. It's only the first few months that the transformation can be unpredictable. Once your body adapts — and it evidently will, since you survived the initial change — you'll be able to slip in and out of wolf-form with ease.*

*You're insane.* A pause followed, and they padded out of the castle in silence. *People don't become wolves.*

Demi's chuckle emerged as a throaty mewl. *Our people do. Come, let's run. Your shoulder has healed nicely from my blood and the transformation. You can keep up with me.*

He broke into a run, glancing behind him to make sure she accompanied him. In her current emotional state, it seemed prudent to distract her from her worries and burdens. He hoped she would become caught up in the freedom of the run and temporarily forget her questions about what had happened.

But if she didn't run with him, he wouldn't leave her alone. He didn't know if she was likely to attempt something drastic if left to her own devices. He had heard of only a few instances where someone was changed without their consent, and the process usually drove them mad. They ended up as a danger to themselves or others.

She hesitated before finally breaking into a run. When she reached his side, Demi increased his pace, and she matched it. Soon, they were sprinting through the fields and forest. He was trying to outrun his rage with Nikia, and she was trying to outrun her thoughts.

\* \* \* \* \*

Later, long after she had lost track of time, they stopped running. Anca panted heavily, disconcerted by the sensation of her tongue flopping against the outside of her mouth. Every muscle in her body ached, but it was the delicious tingle of exertion, not the pain she had previously experienced from Nikia's bite.

Her vision was sharper than she had ever imagined it could be. She could see an owl perched in a tree as clearly as if it was daylight, and she was able to make out the speckles on its wings and the tiny feathers on its neck.

She could smell everything so vividly that the sense had acquired texture. She could feel the odor of the flowers carried by the breeze, touch the trace of deer droppings wafting to her, and reach out for Demi, whose sexual arousal made her nose twitch.

It matched her own. She wondered how she could ache to have his cock inside her while the terrible weight of the surreal night's events flooded her mind. At that moment, she had a more urgent desire for Demi than she did for a logical explanation of why she was running through the forest in a wolf's body.

Surely, it was all a dream. She cast her eyes to the side to view Demi, who had sprawled on the ground. His sides heaved with exhaustion, and his tongue lolled out of his mouth. He looked like nothing more than a big, cuddly dog.

If she had ever given it much thought, she would have supposed the way one thinks changed when they became a werewolf, but she was discovering it didn't. She was still herself, and each of her thoughts was her own. She wasn't driven by a wild, aimless desire to couple and hunt. Her passion ran deeper than that, motivated by memories of how tender he had been with her the night before. She wanted to feel that again.

She laid down gingerly, not yet accustomed to the change in her anatomy. She misjudged where she planned to land and ended up scooting toward Demi on her belly. The submissiveness in the gesture wasn't lost on her, but she found it sexy, not demeaning. Demi was very much the quintessential Alpha male right now.

When she was lying beside him, Anca nudged his head with her nose, wondering if she was showing him affection or amusing him. A brief image of her doing such things in her human form made her want to simultaneously giggle and cringe with embarrassment.

He put his paw on hers and rubbed his muzzle against hers. His head dipped lower, and he nudged the pendant still hanging around her neck.

She was so used to it that she hadn't realized she had been wearing it when she transformed. It hung low on her chest, and she was suddenly terrified of losing it.

Demi rolled against her, nipping her lightly on the shoulder. Anca responded by swiping her paw against his side. He made a low sound, somewhere between a growl and a purr, and lifted his head to lick her ear.

She shivered at the sensation, finding it as delightful as she did in her human form. She ached with desire, and her inability to make love with him frustrated her.

*We can make love,* he contradicted.

She eyed him skeptically. *How?*

*We can mate in our wolf-form —*

*No!*

Something that sounded like a chuckle gurgled from his throat. *I was going to say, we could do that, but I've never tried it. I was going to suggest we change back.*

*I thought I was stuck like this until sunrise.*

*No. Concentrate on changing and you will.*

She closed her eyes, straining to regain her human form. She felt a shift in her body, but when she opened her eyes, she was still covered with fur, though her muzzle had disappeared.

*Sexy,* he teased as he transformed. "Half-woman and half-wolf. Interesting."

She glowered at him, though she didn't know if her current configuration of features allowed him to get the full impact of her angry expression. "It's hard," she said, and she jumped with surprise at the growl lacing her tone.

He nodded. "Focus. Picture your body changing back. Imagine each cell forming its original shape."

She closed her eyes and allowed him to talk her through the transformation. In a couple of minutes, she was back to being Anca—wearing only the ruby pendant and crouched on a bed of soft grass and rose bay. "This is the most vivid dream I've ever had," she whispered. "It must be that dram Ylenia made me drink—if that wasn't part of the dream."

He quirked a brow. "So, this is all a dream?" He spread out his hands to encompass the forest around them.

"Absolutely," she said with conviction, *needing* to believe it was. "It can't possibly be anything else."

He remained silent—further proof it was a dream, surely.

She reached out for him. "I'm hungry, Demi."

"I could catch something—"

"For you." She raked her eyes over his bare chest. "What I'm dreaming about us doing is preferable to what I'm no doubt really doing."

"What's that?"

"I'm burning up with fever and thrashing in bed. You're probably there to soothe me, which is how you crept into my dreams." She leaned closer, until her lips nearly brushed his. "It's no mystery why I'm dreaming I'm a werewolf. Being bitten by a wolf has obviously influenced my subconscious." Her brow furrowed. "Though I do wonder why I've cast Nikia as the villain in this little melodrama."

"You're perceptive," he said flatly. "Listen, Anca..."

She sensed he was about to dispel her dream theory, so she moved forward to close the remaining distance between them. Her bare breasts pressed against his lightly furred chest when she leaned closer. She touched her lips to his to silence him. She was unprepared for the demanding thrust of his tongue against her mouth as it pushed its way through the barrier to plumb her depths.

Anca shivered as his tongue stroked hers. He was gentle, but there was a hint of roughness to his touch. The combination was exhilarating. She strained against him, opening her mouth wider and flicking the tip of her tongue against the side of his.

Demi pulled back slightly, breathing heavily. "We must talk—"

She put two fingers to his lips. "Shh." She replaced her fingers with her lips, softening her mouth to fit the contours of his. She flicked her tongue across his bottom lip, and his body jerked. She tilted back her neck and moved far enough away to meet his eyes. "I don't want to talk."

He made a growling sound and tangled his hand in her hair. "You look so tempting in the moonlight. The silver gives your skin a pearly sheen."

She traced her finger around his nipple, and then ran her nails through his hair, grazing the side of her own breast. "Do you want me, Demi?"

"Of course."

"I want you too." She shook her head, sending strands of tangled, dark-brown hair flying around her face. "I don't want to think about anything. I don't feel much like talking right now. I only want to feel…you inside me, for a start."

He hesitated, seemingly torn between his need to speak and his need for her.

Anca held her breath, waiting for him to decide. She released it in a harsh sigh when he crushed her against him in a tight embrace and practically slammed his mouth against hers. The wildness of his emotions excited her, and she eagerly returned his kisses.

Her hand slid from his chest to trail down his stomach. She paused to caress the soft skin of his flat stomach before venturing lower. A denser growth of curls covered his cock, and she fluffed it before grasping his cock. He froze as she circled the head and squeezed gently. He was hard and pulsing.

Moisture pooled between her thighs as her body signaled it was prepared for him. "I've never met anyone who arouses me so quickly," she said after she broke the kiss. She drew in a deep breath and regained a measure of control. "Just the thought of making love with you gets me hot."

He looked pleased by her comment. "It is the same for me. Until last week, I hadn't seen you except in a faded photograph your mother sent years ago, but I dreamed of you each night. I fantasized about touching every inch of you."

"And being touched?" Anca asked with a throaty purr and squeezed his cock again.

"Oh, yes. Sometimes, I thought I would go mad with the need to hold you. The waiting seemed interminable, but I was able to alleviate some of the frustration by imagining how good you would feel when we were finally joined." He cupped her cheek in his hand as the hand in her hair began to smooth and separate the strands.

A dart of jealousy surprised her. "I'm sure other women provided temporary relief," she said in a biting tone. She winced at her reaction, again surprised. She had always subscribed to the rule of leaving past relationships in the past. It disconcerted her to be jealous of other women he had held.

Demi shook his head. "There were no others, *meu dragostia*." He spoke proudly, without a trace of embarrassment, as some men might have displayed with such a revelation.

She blinked, certain she hadn't understand. "I'm sorry...what?"

"I have never touched another woman." He dropped his hand from her cheek to touch his chest, thumping his finger lightly over his heart. "Always, you were here and in the back of my mind, guiding my choices."

She swallowed, and her brow furrowed with confusion. "I don't understand. You said you hadn't even seen me, except in an old picture. How can that be?"

Demi shrugged. "My heart has always known you. You're my lifemate, Anca. The choice to consummate our union was always yours, but there was never a time I didn't love you."

Anca shook her head. "This doesn't make any sense. You're saying you're a virgin?"

He nodded. "I was until last night."

She started, having temporarily forgotten about their lovemaking in the wake of his revelation. "So, you waited for me because you knew we were destined for each other, even knowing I might reject you?" There was more than a hint of uncertainty in her voice as she struggled to comprehend what he was telling her.

The corners of his mouth curved in a small smile. "That's correct." A shadow crossed his eyes. "I don't expect you to have done the same. You grew up in a different world, not living by our ways."

She rubbed her eyes. "Are you saying all Corsovans save themselves for their destined lifemates?"

He bit his lip. "No, not exactly. Only a few have a lifemate. Tradition dictates the Protector of Corsova should have one, so their reign is a shared burden."

Anca sighed. "Save all the mumbo-jumbo about tradition, please. I'm still reeling from the shock of your innocence."

He frowned. "Why does this shock you?"

"Well, you must be about forty — "

"Thirty-seven," he interjected.

"How could you have remained innocent for so long? It's not in anyone's nature. The men I know would die if they were virgins at your age. And you can forget about any of them openly admitting it."

Demi shrugged. "It is accepted and encouraged in our country. I feel no shame in the admission." His spine straightened. "I am proud to have my body know only yours."

Tears sparkled in her eyes, and she blinked them back. A feeling of guilt for having not stayed pure stirred in her breast, and she shoved it down. The tradition was archaic, she reminded herself.

A twinkle of amusement glinted in his eyes. "Besides, pure and innocent are two different things, Anca. I have had years to learn everything I need to know to make our lovemaking pleasurable. I may lack hands-on experience, but I have the knowledge."

She chuckled at his words, relieved he had made the effort to lighten the atmosphere. "I suppose you want to get your hands on me, huh?"

Demi put his hand on her thigh and squeezed gently. "Yes." He slid his hand higher, until his fingers brushed against her pussy. "Will you open for me?"

Anca felt entranced as she parted her thighs and lay back down on the dew-moistened grass. She could barely comprehend what Demi had told her. How could he possibly have been a virgin until the previous night? She shook her head with wonder as his finger probed her pussy and flicked over her clit. He certainly had applied himself to learning, she thought with a half-smile.

She parted her thighs wider to allow his hand to cover her pussy. He rotated his palm in a slow, circular motion as he brought his other hand up to part her folds. Her breath hissed through her teeth as he thrust a finger inside her pussy. His thumb circled her clit, pressing gently in time with the rhythm of his finger thrusting in and out of her.

Anca lifted her head to look at him. He knelt between her parted thighs, intent on pleasing her. She stretched her arm to run her fingers down his forearm. "You're too far away," she complained with a smile.

Demi looked up and a grin curved across his mouth. "I can be much closer, *dragostia*, if that is your wish."

She nodded, expecting him to lie beside her. Instead, he sprawled on his stomach and put his mouth on her stomach. His hot breath on her navel caused her pussy to clench, and a liquid rush of arousal accompanied it. She instinctively arched her hips as his mouth slid lower.

Demi rubbed his cheek against her smooth pussy lips. "Do you always keep your pussy bare?"

"I try to." She bit her lip as his tongue snaked out to trace her swollen lips. "Oh, God, Demi," she said with a moan.

"Does this please you?" His voice was a whisper against her sensitive skin, causing her nerve endings to tingle with awareness.

"Yes." Anca managed to concentrate long enough to provide a simple answer. "More."

Demi complied with her request. One of his hands slipped from her pussy to squeeze her thigh, but the other pushed her lips farther apart. Seconds later, the warm caress of his breath against her clit caused her whole body to spasm with pleasure. Anca pushed up her hips, silently demanding he touch her pussy with his mouth.

He nipped her clit gently, but didn't linger. Instead, his tongue swept a path below her clit and down the cleft of her pussy to probe her opening. His nose brushed against her clit, and he inhaled. His indrawn breath made her tremble with need.

Anca squirmed as his moist tongue darted inside her. She groaned aloud when he flicked his tongue quickly, shallowly sweeping the inner walls of her pussy. She tangled her hands in his hair. "Where did you learn this?" Her voice was husky with passion, and she was panting.

He didn't answer. Instead, Demi pushed the thigh he held wider and burrowed deeper into her pussy. His tongue went deep inside and stroked her slowly. The hand keeping her lips parted shifted, and his thumb circled around her clit, but didn't actually touch the sensitive bud.

She whimpered at the delicious torture he inflicted. Her breathing was ragged, and she could feel her lower body tightening, preparing for release. She tried to thrust against him, but found herself anchored by his firm hold on her thigh. "Please."

He chuckled, and the vibrations swept through her pussy, triggering small convulsions. Anca could feel the walls of her pussy spasming around his tongue as he applied more pressure and surged even deeper. She moaned as he slid his thumb across her clit as he circled it. He pressed lightly and flicked his tongue inside her, causing her arousal to flood his mouth and her pussy to contract with her orgasm.

She tightened her hold on his hair as her body shook with waves of satisfaction. His tongue continued to caress her as she spasmed around him, and she cried out as the pleasure intensified, causing her pussy to contract more violently. Her nipples ached, and her stomach quivered. She arched her hips frantically against him as she reached a crescendo.

Slowly, her orgasm dissipated, leaving her weak and breathing heavily. She became aware of clutching his hair and loosened her hold. He lifted his head, and his mouth glistened with proof of her pleasure. Her hand shook as she reached for him. He settled his body gently over hers and rested his head between her breasts.

"Your heart's racing."

"Uh huh," she managed to say. When he shifted slightly, his hard cock brushed against her thigh, and she parted her legs wider. "Let's get your heart rate raised," she said in a teasing tone.

He hesitated. "I have no protection."

Anca did a quick mental calculation. "Well, it should be a safe time of the month, and obviously you're in good health since, well, you know... So was I at my last physical, a few months ago. I haven't had a lover for a few years, until you. It's okay to make love."

Again, Demi hesitated, and then shook his head. "No. We can't risk making you pregnant."

An image of holding his child flashed through her mind, and it had the substance of a vision, not the illusions of her imagination. A wave of maternal sentiment surprised her. "Our baby—"

"It isn't time," he interrupted as he pressed his forehead against hers. "Someday, yes, but right now it's too risky, with the—" Demi broke off abruptly.

She bit her lip, considering the suggestion hovering on the tip of her tongue. She had always been curious about it. Would he want to...?

Demi's eyes widened with surprise, and he lifted his head to stare into her eyes. "You would be willing to try such a thing?"

Anca shrugged and avoided answering by asking, "Are you always going to be poking in my mind?"

He laughed. "No. It's a reaction to our intimacy and the experiences we've shared tonight. Your telepathic powers have increased in the last few hours. Can't you feel it?"

She closed her eyes and concentrated. Soon, she felt a surge of power and knew he was right. She had gained mental strength since her transformation to wolf-form. She wondered if her visions would be more reliable and sharper in the future. Demi interrupted her speculation.

*Do you want me to make love to you in such a fashion?*

Somehow, it was easier to discuss the idea with thoughts, rather than words. Anca squeezed her eyes shut more tightly and focused on her thoughts. *I'm curious, but frightened. It might hurt.*

*I'm sure it will, at first. We don't have to do anything if you aren't ready. We can return to the castle if you prefer. I have protection in my chambers.*

She hesitated, torn between curiosity and caution. His mind brushed against hers, and his excitement and wonder transferred to her as he pictured them joined. She felt his cock spasm against her thigh when he imagined entering her, and his desire was an echo of hers. "I want you to make love to me." Verbalizing the request gave it more impact. She swallowed back her fear as Demi leaned back to kneel between her legs.

"Thank you for trusting me." His tone was almost reverent. "I'll be gentle. If you want to stop…"

She nodded and forced a smile, reminding herself that millions of couples practiced anal sex. It must be enjoyable to have gained such a following, for surely there weren't that many masochists in the world.

"I've studied the technique." He grasped her thighs and pulled her higher onto his lap.

"I've thought about it, but I've never done it before," she said in a wobbly voice. Her smile felt a little jittery, but she clung to it as Demi parted her pussy and covered his fingers with her natural lubrication. She held her breath as he trailed his finger down to her anus and rubbed gently against the opening.

His caresses were soft and slow, and he paused frequently to wet his fingers. Anca relaxed under the gentle massage and barely felt anything when his finger entered her anus. He wiggled his finger gently, and she stiffened when she felt a flash of pain, accompanied by a stir of pleasure.

He must have sensed when her muscles relaxed again, because he eased a second finger inside her after sliding it in her pussy to moisten it. He thrust his fingers carefully, and Anca squirmed. There was a twinge of discomfort, but enjoyment of the sensation outweighed it. Was it pleasure from the physical sensation, or more from the implied taboo of doing such a thing? She didn't care to analyze it.

When Demi withdrew his fingers as his other hand probed her pussy, she knew he was about to enter her. She struggled to relax, knowing it would make the process easier. He teased her clit for too brief a moment, causing her to writhe upwards against his hand.

A few seconds passed when he didn't touch her, and she resisted the urge to lift her head to watch him prepare. She focused on her breathing and recapturing the thrill of experimentation. Despite her resolve, she stiffened when he adjusted their position and his cock head rested against her anus.

"It isn't too late to change your mind." His tone was soothing, and he stopped moving.

"No, I want to."

"Relax then, *meu dragostia*." Demi's finger slid over her clit in soothing circles as his cock pressed into her back passage. His other hand guided his cock into her, and he continued to stroke her clit as he moved past her resistance and entered her a few inches.

His cock was definitely different from his fingers, she thought with a pained grimace. There was more pain and a sense of almost uncomfortable fullness. If her pussy hadn't started spasming from his tender ministrations, she might have told him to stop right then.

"Tell me when to move," Demi whispered. "You're in complete control. If you want me to withdraw, I will immediately."

She nodded, squeezing her lids tightly closed. Anca waited for the pain to pass, and it did a short time later. The sense of fullness remained, but it was starting to feel good. Coupled with the way he rubbed her clit, the sensation intensified her arousal. "You could try thrusting."

His movements were slow and careful, and he continued to massage her pussy. The first thrust hurt worse than his initial penetration, but each subsequent thrust brought more pleasure than pain. As he maintained his slow pace and rubbed her clit, he spoke soothing words to her in Corsovan.

Anca was soon squirming with pleasure, thrusting upward against his fingers as she clenched her buttocks. Each time she did so, she heard him grunt. When she opened her eyes, she saw sweat beaded his forehead, and his face appeared flushed in the moonlight. It was obvious his control was tenuous, as was hers.

She cupped her neglected breasts and rubbed the aching nipples. He seemed to sense her urgency, because his thrusts got deeper and faster, and he applied a hint of pressure to her clitoris as he rolled it between his thumb and forefinger.

His orgasm came scant seconds before hers, causing his body to stiffen as his cock spasmed. When he cried out, his voiced pleasure intensified hers. Anca arched her hips up at a sharp angle as she came. He followed the movements of her body, burying his cock inside her and spurting the last traces of his satisfaction. He continued to stroke her clit, but his pace had slowed as her juices made his fingers slick again.

The spasms racking her lower body faded, and she felt his cock soften inside her anus. She winced as he withdrew carefully, surprised by a bit of pain after all the pleasure. "I never expected that," she confessed. "I didn't think it would feel so good."

Demi nodded as he rolled onto his side and settled beside her. He put his arm across her waist. "Neither did I. I've heard unpleasant things about making love like this. Yet, now I wonder how one can't find pleasure in doing this. You were so tight around my cock. I never imagined…" He trailed off with a sigh. "I find myself needing to rest before we return to the castle. You have exhausted me with your wanton ways."

Her grin disappeared behind a yawn. When it passed, Anca bit her lip. "If I'm dreaming, none of this happened."

"If you aren't, it all happened," he countered in a sleepy tone.

Anca sighed. "I don't know how I feel about that." She laid her head on his chest and curved her body against his. "I don't want to undo anything between us, but if this happened, that means it all did. It's all real."

"Yes." His voice was fuzzy and distant, indicating he was almost asleep. "All real," he repeated.

Anca swallowed a lump in her throat. It must all be a dream, she decided. After all, she had never had the courage to admit to her secret curiosity before. No doubt, she would awaken tomorrow morning in the castle and discover none of this had happened. "No doubt," she said softly, struggling to keep her whispered tone firm. She ignored the dart of doubt accompanying the thought and allowed sleep to claim her.

# Chapter Ten

"It's not a dream." Anca groaned as she sat up, noticing the sky had lightened, though the sun had yet to rise. She was still beside Demi on the ground, completely nude, and aching as though she had been thoroughly made love to after running a marathon—which was pretty much what had happened to her last night.

Demi propped his chin on his hand and gave her a small smile. "No, not a dream."

She shook her head, refusing to believe everything that had happened yesterday. Her shock deepened when Demi transformed to a large, silvery-white wolf.

*Hurry and change so we can make it back to the castle. Ylenia has much to discuss with you.*

Last night, she hadn't paid much attention to the mechanics of Demi speaking inside her mind, but this morning she was aware of the low buzzing in her head. It was more of a vibration than a sound.

How could it be? Demi was a werewolf? She was a werewolf? Anca shook her head again, attempting to dismiss the fantastical notion. She must still be dreaming.

His chuckle emerged as a pleasant growl. *We aren't werewolves. We've formed an alliance with their kind. Don't you remember what I told you last night?*

A wave of nausea accompanied Anca's reluctant nod as their conversation came back to her. "What are we then?" she asked the question mechanically, still not able to believe what had happened. She must still be feeling the effects of the wolf biting her. Right now, she was probably raving in a fevered state. Wasn't she? How could it be otherwise?

Demi shook his massive, furry head. *It falls to your father or Ylenia to explain.*

*Please tell me!* she responded with thought as naturally as she would have spoken to anyone else. The realization brought her up short, making her question her assumption that she was still dreaming

He shook his head again. *Transform, dragostia. Time is short.*

Anca closed her eyes and concentrated on becoming a wolf. Last night's transformation was a hazy recollection, and she couldn't remember how she had done it. How could she even attempt to do it, unless she believed even a smidgeon of what her eyes had shown her and Demi told her. With a sense of discomfort at the attempt, she struggled to complete the process, more than half-convinced she would never be able to.

Her skin felt stretched thin, and every nerve in her body ached, but that was the only side effect she noticed of her attempt to transform. It was nothing like the pain she had experienced last night. She sighed at the futility of the attempt and opened her eyes to tell Demi she couldn't do it.

She looked down and saw her muzzle. Anca blinked, closed her eyes, waited a few seconds, and opened them again. She craned her neck and saw she had transformed. The reality of the situation crashed on her, and she knew she couldn't deny what was happening to her—what had happened. Somehow, she had the ability to become a wolf.

If that was real, then everything was real. If she accepted this, she had to accept it was all true. Could she do that?

Her mind shied away from her heavy thoughts to concentrate on something more mundane. *Why didn't it hurt like last night?*

*Your body has accepted the change. You'll never experience more than mild discomfort again. In time, that too will fade, as transforming becomes second nature.*

*How long will that take?*

*Years, maybe.*

He padded away from her, leaving Anca little choice but to follow. She didn't want to be lost again. He set an easy pace, and her tight muscles loosened as they ran through the trees and fields.

As she ran beside Demi, she couldn't deny what had happened any longer. Her life had taken an unexpected turn, and that was putting it mildly. Believing everything Demi had told her was one thing. Accepting it was quite another.

\* \* \* \* \*

When they arrived back at the castle, Anca was surprised when Demi didn't slip back into his human form. She stopped abruptly, cocking her head. *Shouldn't we go back to…us?*

*Why?*

*What if someone sees us like this?*

Demi's ears flickered in the early morning breeze. *They will think nothing of it. However, the future queen and her lifemate strolling nude into Castle Draganescu might raise a few eyebrows.*

One advantage to being a wolf was her blush didn't show. Anca settled for nodding her head, disconcerted by the way her skin rolled when she did so. Her tongue emerged to pant, and she drew it back in her mouth quickly. As she did so, she raked it across her fangs, a vivid reminder of the physical changes accompanying her new ability.

She followed Demi in through the kitchen. No one gave them a second look. She found herself sniffing as she walked past the oven, and was again disconcerted by the way her tail started wagging as if on autopilot. Anca hoped she wouldn't retain any wolf traits when she returned to her true form.

Demi escorted her to her chambers and followed her inside. As soon as the door closed behind them, he slipped back into his human form. Anca did the same, once again taking a moment to concentrate on the act.

He leaned forward and kissed her quickly. "Dress and be prepared for Ylenia's summons. She'll send someone to escort you to her. It will probably be soon, as she rises early."

Anca nodded, resisting the urge to wind her arms around Demi's neck and hold him close to her. She longed for a means of escaping her fear, but didn't think she would find it with him. The only way to reject the changes was to return to New York and not look back. A pang in her chest dismissed the notion. She couldn't stand the thought of leaving Demi without things resolved between them. Moreover, she still hadn't gotten to know her father.

He stroked her cheek. "I love you. If it was possible, I would be there for your meeting with Ylenia."

"Please come," she whispered.

"I can't. Your father will surely wish to speak to me about what happened to you yesterday, and Ylenia will prefer privacy." He kissed her again before stepping away and assuming wolf-form. He padded to the door and touched it lightly with his paw.

It took her a few seconds to realize he wanted the door opened. It had closed tightly, and he wasn't able to pry it open with his paw. She opened it for him, shielding herself behind the door to hide her state of undress. As the door closed behind him, a heavy sense of pressure filled her, and she ran to the bathroom to vomit.

Once she had emptied her stomach of its meager contents, Anca dropped to the cool stone floor and curled into a ball. So many thoughts whirled in her mind that she couldn't concentrate on any of them for long—even the most life-altering events, like now having increased psychic powers and the ability to transform into a wolf at will.

Anca pushed herself off the floor and turned on the faucets to fill the large tub. She tried clearing her mind of all the confusing thoughts and simply getting through the morning. Without being told, she knew the meeting with Ylenia would hold more revelations, and faced the prospect with dread, knowing she couldn't escape learning the truth, even if she wanted to. As she had heard several times, it was her destiny.

* * * * *

A young woman with light-brown hair came for her an hour later. The girl curtsied, causing the hem of her white robe to fan out across the floor. "Your Highness, I'm here to bring you to Ylenia."

Anca nodded, feeling incapable of speech. She followed the silent girl from her room and through the castle. Today, she remembered where some of the halls led and knew they were going into the tapestry room before the girl opened the door.

A tea tray rested on the small table in the corner. Two empty chairs faced each other across the table. No one was in the room, except them.

The girl curtsied again. "Ylenia will arrive shortly." She turned to leave, and then spun around quickly. "I'm sorry, m'lady."

Anca frowned. "For what?"

"I was your guard, assigned by Lord Nicodemus. If I had done my duty yesterday, you would have been safe." Tears glittered in her large amber eyes. "Please forgive me."

The girl seemed perilously close to throwing herself to the ground and hugging Anca's legs. She smiled at the girl. "Don't give it another thought. It wasn't your fault. I thought I would be safe with my sister."

The girl's bowed head prevented her expression from being seen, but her body language suggested she wanted to say something about that assumption. Apparently, she reined in the impulse, because all she said was, "Thank you, m'lady. You're very kind." Once again, the girl started to leave.

"Wait. What's your name?"

"Starr." With a quick curtsey, she hurried from the room.

Anca shook her head, realizing she had met Starr before, during her arrival at the castle. She had been one of the wolves curled by the fire. What a strange place

Corsova was. She wondered how many others she had met in their various forms, and then wondered how many varieties of forms she might find among the citizenry.

She tried to dismiss her musings by turning her attention to the tapestries. A few of the hangings depicted scenes in nature or fiercely scowling leaders—male and female—in various finery from the ages, but a significant number portrayed a more violent history.

There was a tapestry showing the throat of a maiden ripped open by a tall man with dark hair. She didn't seem to mind the blood flowing down her skin and into his mouth, if one judged by her sated expression. A shiver of mingled fear and desire seized Anca. She tore her gaze from it to examine the others, letting the images blur together, until she arrived at a particularly large one displayed prominently on the far wall.

It showed two women and a man standing in a semi-circle around a dais. A golden chalice rested on the dais, and the younger man and woman of the trio each had a hand around the base. Blood stained the cuffs of their dress and shirt. The older woman's wrist was slashed open, and her blood appeared to be filling the goblet. A red moon shone brightly through the window displayed in the corner of the tapestry.

The picture evoked strange emotions in Anca—dread, longing, and a flash of memory. She reached out a hand to trace the chalice she recognized from the vision she had received the night Demi came to her shop. That seemed like a lifetime ago.

"Careful, dear. That one is hundreds of years old, and the thread is weak. Even restoration hasn't completely salvaged it." Though the woman's voice was rough, there was an underlying softness to her tone.

Anca turned to eye the woman who she guessed to be Ylenia. She was a modest five-two, if even, with a chubby build, wildly curling salt-and-pepper hair bound in a precarious knot, and a white robe embroidered with tiny yellow roses at the neckline and hem. She didn't appear impressive enough to be the spiritual leader of an entire culture.

She winked at Anca, as though reading her thoughts. "Come sit with me, dear. We have much to discuss."

Anca walked forward, taking the seat across from Ylenia as the older woman settled into one. She watched as Ylenia poured two cups of tea into bone china cups, sans handles, and passed one to her. She eyed it uncertainly. "What's in this?" She had vague memories of drinking something noxious the night before.

"Simple oolong, Anca." Her eyes twinkled with amusement. "I find tea settles my nerves better than any spirits your father might enjoy."

She picked up the cup and swirled the contents, but didn't drink. "Should I be nervous?"

One of Ylenia's shoulders moved in a half-shrug. "I don't know. I've never been in this situation myself. Always when counseling the next leader, they knew what to expect."

Anca shook her head. "Expect from what?"

"The Blood Oath." Ylenia sipped her tea after adding a sugar cube. "I'm getting ahead of myself. Valdemeer tells me you have no idea who we are…what you are."

"Demi keeps saying 'our people'," she said softly, finally sipping the tea. It was strong enough to be bracing, but lacked the bitter aftertaste that often accompanied tea steeped too long.

"We're vampires, dear."

She spat out the drink when she choked. Anca struggled to draw in a deep breath as the coughing fit peaked and passed. Would she ever adjust to the blasé attitude of the residents of Corsova? She could understand if they were all delusional, but what had happened to her disproved that comforting theory. She couldn't doubt Ylenia's sincere belief, which meant she had to either accept what she was hearing or run away. She sighed, wondering why she found it so easy to believe, but so difficult to embrace.

Ylenia smiled. "I know it's difficult for you, since you've been raised in the ways of humans. Had your mother kept you in Corsova, you would have never known another way. You wouldn't doubt the veracity of my statement."

"I would have been brainwashed, you mean?" Anca asked harshly, although she didn't really believe any of the citizens had been indoctrinated in this lifestyle. As difficult as it was to admit, it seemed to be their natural state. That didn't mean she wanted it to be second nature for her.

Ylenia didn't bother to retort. "It's a shame you lost so much of your heritage, but Katrine did what was necessary to save your life."

"I think she saved more than my life." Anca set down the cup with a clink. "She saved my sanity too."

A reproachful look appeared in Ylenia's eyes. "Now, dear, don't be like that. We aren't insane or brainwashed." She shrugged. "We are what we are, which happens to be vampires. You know I speak the truth, but you want to shy away from your destiny."

It seemed imperative to continue to deny her place in their madness. She challenged Ylenia with her chin tilted and her voice icy. "If you're vampires, why don't you have any of the classic signs: intolerance of daylight, ingestion of blood, and the like?"

Ylenia laughed. "Vampires aren't quite the way the world fancies them to be, Anca...at least not all vampires. We can move freely in sunlight and moonlight, we are able to eat food, as long as we supplement our diet with blood—hence the "special" Corsovan wine served with every meal. We aren't immortal, but we are long-lived." She tilted her head. "If you were in a lighter mood, I'd ask you to guess my age. I bet you would never say one-hundred-and-four."

Anca shook her head, not convinced. "So, where does the blood for the *wine* come from? I don't see stacks of peasants' bodies outside the walls of the castle."

"Not every citizen in Corsova is a vampire—"

"Yeah, there're werewolves too," she muttered under her breath.

With a disapproving look, Ylenia said, "Our country is a haven—"

"So I've heard." She struggled to maintain an even tone, knowing losing control wouldn't gain her anything except a temporary reprieve from the knowledge she had obtained...knowledge she had never wanted and yearned to escape from.

"Humans also live inside our borders. In exchange for our protection, they're happy to keep us supplied with blood."

"Happy to, or afraid not to?" Anca asked archly.

A hint of anger darkened Ylenia's eyes. "We don't believe in unnecessary violence. We're as civilized as humanity these days," she said with a hint of sarcasm.

"It's a grave offense to kill any human on our lands, and the ruler metes out punishment accordingly. Before Illiana, no vampire had taken the life of a human in hundreds of years." Lines creased her face. "Unfortunately, she seemed to revel in bloodlust. She was also good at keeping her proclivities hidden, or Valdemeer would have stopped her much sooner."

Her brow furrowed at the unexpected twist in the conversation. "Who's Illiana?"

"Nikia's mother. That is for your father to tell you about, if he wishes. I didn't mean to deviate from our topic." Ylenia set down the cup she'd been holding but not drinking from. "My duty is to tell you of your past and future. In ancient times, we were all vampires, and the blood we needed came from the animals we hunted. As time passed, more and more stopped practicing our ways and became human. As the world changed around us, we turned to a new source of sustenance."

A sad expression settled on her face. "Our kind is few and outnumbered. We must always carefully guard our secret, lest we be eradicated by those who would fear us."

Anca sat in stunned silence, finding it more difficult to reject what she was hearing in the wake of the old woman's conviction. More than that, on an instinctive level, she recognized the truth in Ylenia's words. Memories of people long dead flowed through her mind, showing her the way things had been.

Ylenia's eyes closed slightly. "Yes, you can sense them. Your link to our ways is strong and growing stronger each day."

Anca shook her head. "No. You're wrong. I won't be stuck here. I know what you want from me, but I'm going back to New York."

"You will turn your back on your father and your people? Your heritage?" Her tone dropped to a whisper. "On Nicodemus? You will abandon your destiny, and for what? Scratching out an existence in an overcrowded city, always yearning for home? Once you set foot on our land, it became part of you. It is the way of things."

"This isn't what I want."

"People cursed with responsibility seldom want it. Only those strong enough to embrace it survive their destinies." Ylenia sighed. "You are destined to become the next Protector of our people. The stars were in alignment on the night of your birth, and the blood-moon draws near. Only you can take the Blood Oath."

Anca swallowed at the firm words, finding the words of rejection trapped in her throat. Her voice was a timid whisper when she asked, "What is the Blood Oath?"

"There is a price for everything." Ylenia sighed again, and her age seemed more visible suddenly. "How it began has been lost in time, but for most of the history of our people, the Blood Oath has heralded the changing of Protectors. Valdemeer is currently charged with guarding our race, but he grows old and tired." Her expression became pinched. "I fear he won't survive another forty-six years until the blood-moon returns. That's why it's imperative you complete the ritual this time."

"I still don't understand. What does it do?"

"It can be a heavy burden, to be marked for the Blood Oath. Much is asked of the Protector of our people. Once the ritual changes you, you become more like the vampire you're familiar with. Sunlight kills you, aging slows even further, and you must never leave your lands. You're tied to each drop of water in the lake, each flower blooming on the mountains, each animal running through the forest, and to the very soil of Corsova. To be without it would cause your death."

Anca blinked. "What? Why?"

"It sustains and regenerates you, as does the presence of our people." Ylenia picked up her cup and took a sip of the tea before continuing. "In return for your sacrifice, you are given two things of value. The first is a lifespan as great as three hundred years. Valdemeer is nearing two hundred-seventy-eight, but he grows tired."

She swallowed at the fantastical statement, somehow unable to muster the ability to refute it. "And the second?"

"Each Protector has a destined lifemate who undergoes the ritual too. Their life is prolonged, and the burden is shared by two." A soft smile creased her mouth. "Nicodemus had grown impatient for Valdemeer to send for you. From the time he was a child, he has pestered me with questions about you — even before you were born. He was often frustrated by my lack of answers."

Anca's eyes widened. Several of Demi's cryptic statements suddenly made sense. "I can reject him though, can't I?"

Ylenia looked displeased with the idea, but she nodded. "Of course. I have never known of any Protector to do so, but it is possible. Do you wish to?"

Anca made a non-committal sound as her heart lurched at the idea of refusing Demi. Another question came to her. "So my mother was Valdemeer's lifemate?"

Ylenia shook her head. "No. Destiny chose Madra for him. I never knew her, but I've heard she was a gentle soul and full of kindness. He adored her very much, and they were happy together for more than a century. When she finally conceived, I've heard they hosted a month-long celebration."

She frowned. "Then how did he end up with Nikia's mother, and later married to mine?"

"Madra died of a mysterious illness." Ylenia's expression tightened. "It wasn't until much later it was discovered she had been poisoned. Valdemeer was heartbroken when his wife and heir died, still in the womb, and he vowed never to marry again, despite his obligation to produce the next Protector."

Ylenia refilled her cup, though she couldn't have drank more than half of it during their conversation. She automatically added more to Anca's cup too. "Illiana was an ambitious woman, and the details of her machinations are sordid. I'll leave the decision to tell you about it to the king."

Anca tapped her fingers impatiently against the table. "Yes, but how did he end up marrying my mother?"

"Katrine's father was a close friend of Valdemeer. He made the match when your mother was but a little child. I remember how terrified she was when she came for the pledging ceremony." Ylenia smiled, lost in memories for a moment. "I was still an acolyte then, and my duties became entertaining your mother so she wouldn't cry."

"Did he love Mother?"

Ylenia sighed. "He had a deep affection for her. He loved her as much as he could, but Valdemeer's heart will always be bound to Madra."

"My mother was okay with that?" She sniffed indignantly. "No wonder she left him."

"Katrine loved your father deeply, and she accepted he was only doing his duty to provide an heir by marrying her. He treated her well, if a bit distantly. After the death of Julian, they became closer, and things were easier for her." Ylenia scowled. "For a time."

"Who's Julian?"

Ylenia looked surprised. "Your mother never told you?"

Anca shook her head.

"He was your brother. If he hadn't died in infancy, the Protectorate of Corsova would have gone to him."

She was so shocked she couldn't breathe for a moment. She'd had a brother, and her mother never thought to mention it? She found it impossible to mourn for the sibling she had never known, but had no trouble summoning bitter resentment. If fate hadn't been so cruel, he would be the one thrust into this position. "How did he die?"

Ylenia paled, and she seemed to find the tea in her cup engrossing. "It was your mother who first suspected. Little hints that became threats, her behavior, and her violent fits when your mother and father conceived you led Katrine to the deduction."

"What deduction?" she asked with dread.

"Your baby brother was poisoned by one who wanted the throne." She shook her head. "Such malice in one so young…"

"Who?" She knew the answer even as she asked the question.

"Nikia. She admitted to it after Katrine fled to protect you. She told Valdemeer she wouldn't rest until she had killed you too, and the 'baby maker', as she called Katrine." Ylenia shivered, though the room was warm. "I've never seen such hatred and determination in anyone, especially not a child."

Anca's stomach heaved, threatening to reject the sip of tea. The realization of how close she had come to death yesterday bore down on her with an almost physical weight. A new appreciation of what her mother had sacrificed to save her filled her, followed by blistering anger directed at Valdemeer. "Why didn't my father do something?"

"What could he do? She is his daughter, and his guilt over how he feels about her has always crippled him when dealing with Nikia."

Ylenia's voice fell to a whisper. "He hated her as a child. He hates her now, knowing what she's done. Yet, he loves her too, because she is his child. Bringing you home would have meant the death of another of his children. It would have been impossible to keep you safe all the time if she was around. Sending her away assured nothing, and the only other solution was to kill her."

Anca's drew in her breath sharply at the stark pronouncement.

"That wasn't a solution either. Can you imagine ordering a death sentence for a six-year-old? Even if his subjects could get past the barbarity of such an act, Valdemeer wouldn't have been able to live with himself."

Tears sparkled in her eyes. "Your parents both gave up a great deal to protect you."

A void inside Anca, left from years of not having two parents, slowly filled, despite her efforts to stay the rush of warmth sweeping through her. Tears burned behind her eyes, and she took shallow breaths. Along with the love came a sense of responsibility. She owed them both for everything they had done.

She tried to resist that thought, knowing if she accepted her role as Valdemeer's heir that her life would change irrevocably. She didn't want to spend the rest of it—especially three hundred years' worth—looking over her shoulder, wondering when Nikia would plot against her again. Nor could she stand the thought of sentencing anyone to death, especially not a family member, when they had been in such short supply all her life.

She sighed heavily and bowed her head.

"You have much to think about, dear." Ylenia returned her cup to the tray. "I'll leave you now."

"Wait." Anca lifted her head. "What happens during this Blood Oath?"

"When the phase of the moon is right and the stars are in alignment, you will gather in the tower, where an orb draws in the rays of the moon, absorbing power. The pendant draws power from the orb, fueling the transition of power from the old ruler to the new.

"Each of you will put blood into the goblet, and then you and Demi will drink. You will swear to protect our people and honor your duties. Demi will swear to assist and support you. I will witness the ritual and ensure it goes as planned." She pointed to Anca's pendant. "The pendant is an integral part of the ceremony, as it holds the power of our people."

It didn't sound too difficult. She frowned, remembering something Ylenia had said. "You said I was the one destined to take the Blood Oath. What happens if someone else takes it?"

Ylenia's brow furrowed. "I don't know. If it's happened before, it wasn't written down in our history. I imagine the person would die."

She swallowed the lump in her throat. "What if I'm not the right person? What if your wires are crossed, or you made a mistake with the calculations?"

Ylenia shook her head. "No, that's impossible—"

"But what if?" she pressed.

She appeared reluctant to answer. "I guess you would die."

Panic flooded her, and Anca shoved away from the table. Forget familial obligations and indulging archaic rituals. No way in Hell was she risking her life for this. "I won't do it."

"Anca—"

"No!" She spun away from the table and ran from the room, ignoring Ylenia calling her name. She didn't look back as she raced through the corridors, somehow finding the chambers assigned to her. She slammed the door behind her and locked it before hurrying toward the closet. She pulled out her suitcases and tossed them on the bed before frantically tearing clothes from the rack. She wouldn't stay even one more minute, promise to Demi notwithstanding. She believed in freewill, not destiny.

# Chapter Eleven

Demi knocked on her door, but she didn't answer. He tried calling her name, but Anca continued to ignore him. Reluctant to invade her privacy, he finally used the master key to open the door. He didn't know what to expect when he entered her bedchamber.

She sat on the floor with her face buried in the mattress. Her opened cases were on the bed, with clothes strewn across it and the coverlet in a haphazard array. She didn't even look up when he closed the door behind him and walked over to the bed. "Anca?" She still didn't look up, even when he settled on the cool floor beside her. "How are you? Please talk to me."

She lifted her head, and looked at him with red rimmed, swollen eyes. Tear tracks lined her cheeks, and her mouth wobbled. She didn't speak as she fell into his arms, burying her face against his chest.

Demi caressed her tangled hair and murmured soothing words to her. When he realized he was speaking Corsovan out of habit, he switched to English. "I know you're frightened of what's coming, but I'll be with you."

She lifted her head away from his shirt. "I-it-it's too mu-much," she stuttered amid hiccups. "I can't do any of this. I don't want any part of this."

He shook his head. "That isn't true, Anca. I can sense your confusion and doubt, but I also feel your longing. You know what you are, and you know what you're destined to be. It's all right to be frightened."

"I'm going home, Demi." She bowed her head, refusing to meet his eyes. "I tried, but I can't give my father what he wants. I can't even give you what you want from me."

He nudged up her chin. "All I want is your love. If you decide to turn your back on your heritage, I'll still be beside you—if you want me."

She sighed. "Of course I do." Her eyes were haunted. "On some level, I feel like I've always known you. That's why it was so easy to fall—" She broke off abruptly, pursing her lips.

Demi pulled her more completely into his arms and began rubbing her back in small circles, trying to ignore the dart of pain from her refusal to speak of her love for him. "All will be well. You'll see. Just give it some time—"

She shook her head. "No. I'm going home. It's time for me to get back to my real life and away from all this craziness."

Demi sighed. "If you want to go back to New York, that's where we'll go. I won't pretend that's the decision I want you to make though. Moreover, I know you don't want to hear it, but your place is here. Part of you is tied to the land now—"

"I refuse to believe that," she said stridently. "I belong in New York, with my mother. I'm not supposed to be a vampire queen. I want my life to be normal. I want to go back to managing *Dragan's Whimsy*, get married, and have children. I don't want to spend three hundred years looking over my shoulder, wondering who's trying to kill me today." Anca swiped her cheeks impatiently. "I can't stay here."

"Don't leave me. I've waited so long for you. Please, just stay a while longer. See the country for yourself before deciding if you can fill your role as the Protector of Corsova." He crushed her against him, sensing her withdrawal. "I don't want to live without you. I want to be the one who shares your burdens. I'll give you a child as soon as the Blood Oath ceremony is over, if that's what you want."

She pulled away with a small whimper, settling onto her knees beside him, though her upper body still pressed against his. "I don't want a child right this minute, Demi. Nor will I be coerced with the promise of one—"

He shook his head. "I wasn't. The physical changes of the Blood Oath would cause you to miscarry. That's why we must wait until after you make your decision." He framed her face with his hands, staring deeply into her eyes. "I would never try to coerce you, but I will try to convince you to stay. Please, just give me the rest of the month."

Her lips trembled, and she appeared to be weakening. "Well…"

"Please, Anca." He put his arm around her waist, bringing her breasts against his chest. "I need you. We've joined. You have no idea how painful it will be for both of us if we're parted."

Her eyes narrowed. "What do you mean?"

"You accepted me the first time we made love. We're bonded now, you and I." His stomach clenched when he realized she hadn't knowingly accepted him. "Oh, Anca, I'm so sorry. I forgot you don't know our ways. I assumed…" He trailed off, shaking his head. "Nothing can undo our bonding now. Parting would be agony for both of us."

"Damn you! You thought you could trick me into staying here." She hit his chest with her balled up fists. "You're just like everyone else, with your secret agendas."

"Anca." He spoke firmly, hoping to cut through her anger so she would really hear him. "I love you, and I wanted nothing more than to join with you. I had no ulterior motives, except my own selfish needs. I didn't think beyond joining with you. Please believe me." He could hear the note of pleading in his voice, but he wasn't concerned about his pride. It was a small sacrifice if she stayed because he bared his heart.

She was quiet for a long moment, and her hands dug into his chest, as she seemed to get lost in thought. Finally, her body relaxed against his. "I'm sorry. I know you wouldn't..." Anca sighed. "I feel it too. I felt it even before we made love, but now I can't stop thinking about you. I knew you were near even before you knocked on my door."

"I feel you every minute of the day too, *meu dragostia*." He buried his face in her hair, inhaling deeply. His eyes widened when her fingers started toying with the buttons of his shirt. "Anca?"

"I'll stay a week," she said in a whisper. "That's all I'll promise for now."

"It's enough." He would make it enough, he vowed. Once again, his concentration faltered when she slipped her hands inside his shirt to stroke his chest. "Do you want to make love now?"

She nodded, and her hair brushed against his face. "I need you, Demi. You're the only thing in this place that makes any sense…the only thing that seems real…" She lifted her head and touched her lips against his.

Demi returned her kiss, allowing her to set the pace. She seemed to be in no hurry as she thoroughly explored his opened mouth with her probing tongue. He groaned softly as she tweaked his nipple while nibbling on his lower lip. His cock sprang completely to life, and he could feel the warmth of her pussy through the soft cotton of her summer dress. He couldn't wait to touch her skin and moved her far enough away to work his hands between them to cup her breasts. The material of her dress was an intolerable barrier.

Demi moved his hands to the tie at the back of her neck and fumbled with the knot. When it loosened, the dress pooled around her waist, displaying a plain white bra with no straps. Demi broke away from her lips to trail his mouth down her chin and neck. He scooted to face her, lifting her higher against him, until he could put his face between her breasts. He brushed aside the pendant, and it was hot to the touch, responding to the emotions flaring between them.

"Touch me." Anca leaned back into his arms, letting him support her upper body, as her fingers threaded through his hair.

Demi braced her weight with one arm while his other hand fumbled with the discreet clasp of the bra, hidden between her breasts. After what seemed like hours of wrangling with it, the hooks slipped free, and the bra fell away to reveal her perfect breasts.

He brought her with him as he leaned his back against the bed, groaning as she straddled one of his thighs. The warmth of her pussy burned into his leg through the material separating them. She stretched, and her nipple brushed against his lips, teasing him. He brought the hard peak into his mouth, unable to withstand the temptation. As he swirled his tongue around it, he heard her cry out with pleasure. Her hold on his hair tightened until it was almost painful, but he didn't push her away.

Demi nipped her nipple gently and was rewarded by her frantic thrusts against his leg. He slipped his hand into the hem of her dress and pulled it up. Anca parted her thighs further for him, and he stroked her pussy through her cotton panties, brushing his hand against his own leg as he did so.

"I want to feel you inside me, Demi." She spoke in a breathless whisper, indicating she was as excited as he was.

"I long for that too," he said against her nipple. He fastened his mouth on the rigid peak again as he pushed aside the crotch of her panties. When he touched the smooth skin of her pussy lips, he shuddered with desire. His cock twitched and hardened further, pressing against his pants. "Can you help me, Anca? Undo my zipper."

She released his hair and trailed her hands down his body. Demi's breath caught in his throat when she slid down his leg, generating friction between them as she created enough room to get her hands between them. He closed his eyes, counting to regain control, as her fingers tugged at the zipper of his pants. When she freed his cock, he let out a shaky breath and opened his eyes. It turned to a ragged sob when her hands ventured inside his briefs to grasp his cock. He couldn't resist thrusting against her hand as she massaged the head of his cock lightly after pushing his briefs below his testicles.

Anca squirmed against his hand, reminding him to touch her. Demi stroked her pussy, finding her wet and ready for him when he slid two fingers inside her. "In my pocket...protection."

She seemed to go out of her way to brush against his cock when she searched for the condom. The torture seemed to last forever, but she finally removed the small package from his pants. She tore off the wrapper and slid the condom on his cock with confident movements. He was glad to have the assistance, because he wasn't sure his hands were steady enough to do more than rub her clit while holding her against him.

When she finished, Anca shifted from straddling his leg to sitting on his lap, angling her legs around his waist, until her shins encountered the barrier of the bed. He bent his knees to support her, and she inched forward to align their pelvises. Demi leaned back a bit more to give her enough room, and he gritted his teeth as her wet pussy cuddled the length of his cock when she eased herself down on him. She was slow in her efforts to take in all of him, and he could feel perspiration beading his lip and trickling down his back. His cock tightened painfully.

When she had settled on him, she covered every inch of his cock. He groaned when she contracted her pussy to squeeze his cock. He gripped her hips and began lifting her in time with his thrusts. He was beyond slow, teasing strokes. He thrust into her quickly, hearing her cries of pleasure as he surged inside her before withdrawing a few inches to repeat the process.

As he entered her, he could feel her pussy getting warmer and wetter around his cock, even through the thin latex. Demi tossed back his head and closed his eyes, concentrating on lasting long enough to bring her pleasure first. His eyes opened again when he felt Anca's hand moving between them. He glanced down, but couldn't see what she was doing.

It was soon obvious, as he felt the back of her hand brushing rhythmically against his skin. The thought of her touching her clit as he thrust into her caused his cock to spasm painfully. He cried out as he lost all control and spilled his seed.

He surged into her as far as he could go and held her tightly against him. As his orgasm peaked, he felt her pussy convulse around him, and she too cried out. She started thrusting again, and he endured the slight pain against his tender cock, surprised when he started to get hard again.

Before he could attain a complete erection, she collapsed against him, sobbing quietly. Her arms were wrapped around his shoulders, and her forehead rested on the top of his head. Tiny contractions continued to emanate from her pussy, bringing him a combination of pleasure and pain. He wrapped his arms around her back and held her against him, content to stay like that forever, if only they could.

* * * * *

During dinner, Anca sipped cautiously at the wine, finally accepting it was indeed blood. It had a coppery, tangy aftertaste that couldn't be anything else. More disconcerting than the confirmation of Ylenia's assertion was her enjoyment of the drink.

As she consumed more, she was aware of her canines lengthening and sharpening and was reminded of the night she fled from Demi at the train station, when her teeth seemed to get stuck in his hand, before he kissed her so passionately. She couldn't deny her body seemed designed to consume blood, just as it seemed designed to give and receive pleasure from Demi.

"You're very quiet," Valdemeer said from the head of the table. Most of the meal had been spent in silence, as none of the three of them seemed inclined to break it.

She saw Demi's gaze shift between them and guessed his intent to leave before he said anything. She gave him a small smile, but didn't attempt to dissuade him. She couldn't avoid speaking with her father forever, and she had only agreed to stay a week, which meant the discussion must be soon.

"If you've finished your dinner, perhaps you would join me for a game of chess?"

Anca nodded. "I'd be happy to, Papa."

Demi wiped his mouth and stood up. "If you'll excuse me…"

"Good night, Nicodemus."

He inclined his head. "M'lord." Demi turned and offered her a half-bow. "Anca."

She hid the smile trying to force its way onto her face, convinced he would join her later that night. "Good night, Demi."

They followed him from the dining room, but took a different hallway to reach her father's study. Valdemeer poured them each a snifter of brandy before they settled at the chess table. Anca chose white and made the first move, then leaned back and waited for him to begin playing or speaking.

He eyed the board, seemingly in no hurry. "Nikia has been confined to her quarters," he said as he moved his knight, "until I decide what to do with her."

"Hmm." Anca tilted her head, considering each move she could make. It had been a long time since high school, and she hadn't played in years. She finally decided on another cautious move. She repositioned a pawn. "Did she really mean to harm me?"

He stroked his beard and studied the board, seeming to find it easier to avoid her eyes. Finally, he moved a pawn to block her. "I believe she planned to kill you. I feared bringing you back to Corsova for that reason, but time grows short…"

After making her move, Anca said, "The blood-moon." She strove to sound neutral, but a hint of fear crept into her voice.

"Yes, in a couple of weeks now." He touched his rook, but withdrew his hand to move his knight again to capture her pawn. "Once you have taken the Oath, she will have no reason to harm you. It will be too late for her then, and she'll have to accept that."

Anca moved her bishop into alignment with his king. "Check." She took a deep breath, gathering her courage. "What if she doesn't accept it? What will you do then?"

His silence was his answer. He moved his queen forward to protect his king. "Will you take the Oath?"

She hesitated over giving him a blunt rejection. "I haven't decided yet." She moved again.

"Ylenia tells me she said a bit more about Illiana than she planned." He scratched his beard again and tilted his head left, then right. His eyes never wavered from the board.

"Yes. She said you would tell me the story if you wanted me to know."

He sighed and lifted his brandy, seeming to temporarily abandon the game. His eyes finally met hers as he leaned back in his chair. "Illiana was very beautiful. In fact, Nikia strongly resembles her—in appearance, temperament, and personality. There are times when I can't tell them apart."

"You were enamored with her?"

He shook his head. "No, though she didn't hide her interest. Madra was my world, and I knew what an ambitious creature Illiana was. Had I been tempted to stray, she wouldn't have been my choice for a mistress. She was dangerous. Her mother was a witch, you know, and taught her craft to Illiana before her death."

"Then Illiana wasn't a vampire?" The word felt strange on her tongue.

"Oh, she was. Her father was a vampire. While handling matters of state, he met and married Illiana's mother. He brought her with him when he returned to our country, though she never took up our ways. Mostly, Elsa was a good woman, but prone to bouts of melancholy. In those moods, she was like another person. She caused the death of her husband by cursing him in anger. She was about to be banished when she committed suicide."

"Leaving Illiana an orphan?"

He nodded. "Yes. Madra was a tenderhearted woman, and she longed for a child. After nearly a hundred years of trying to conceive, we thought one of us was barren. She brought Illiana to live in the castle and treated her like a daughter." A trace of bitterness appeared in Valdemeer's eyes. "I didn't realize Illiana's affections for Madra were a front until she was older. Even after she tried to seduce me, I couldn't send her away. I couldn't bear to deny Madra anything."

After a long silence and another sip of brandy, Valdemeer said, "It was like a miracle when Madra became pregnant. Our entire kingdom rejoiced. I swear the celebration lasted at least a month."

"But Illiana wasn't pleased, was she?" Anca guessed.

He shook his head. "No. She knew our child had been conceived during the correct moon phase and would be the rightful heir to Corsova. She refused to give up her bid for power, so she slowly poisoned Madra. At first, the healer said she was ill from the pregnancy. As Madra wasted away, her only thoughts were for the baby..." He trailed off.

Anca reached across the chess table to squeeze her father's hand, but she didn't interrupt.

"She died before the child could survive on his own." Tears sparkled in Valdemeer's eyes. "I swore on their grave never to marry again. Illiana was crafty—I'll give her that." He sighed heavily. "She waited more than a year before approaching me again. When I rejected her harshly, she stayed out of my way. I thought my threat to banish her had scared her away."

"What happened?"

He rubbed his eyes. "She drugged me and seduced me, getting herself with child." A harsh laugh escaped him. "She didn't calculate correctly, and there was no way her child could be my heir, because it hadn't been conceived during the right phase of the moon. She still demanded I marry her, and I retaliated by locking her away in one of the turrets with only a deaf-mute woman for an attendant."

"She died in childbirth?"

He nodded. "The attendant didn't notify anyone because she had died of a heart attack days before. It was Illiana's screams of pain that alerted the guards. I rushed to her chamber, hoping to provide a bit of comfort for her. I didn't hate her then, you see. I only mistrusted her."

He paled, and his hands shook when he lifted the glass. "Illiana knew she was dying. She raved on about the murders she had committed—humans who had the misfortune to cross her path, the poor attendant, frightened to death, and Madra. She described her murder in graphic detail, right down to the pain she had endured, especially at the end…"

He shook his head. "If she hadn't been bleeding to death, I would have killed her with my bare hands. Illiana looked at her child, gave a strange smile, and said, 'I like the name Nikia.' Those were her last words before she slipped from this world. She was the child's mother, so I christened her with the name Illiana chose." He hung his head. "I didn't care anything for the child at that time, so what did it matter?" He sighed and raised his head, meeting her gaze. There was a hint of shame in his eyes.

Anca shivered as he finished speaking. "Nikia knows all this?"

He nodded. "I don't know how. I demanded she be protected from the truth about her mother, but someone must have been indiscreet. I soon realized there was nothing to protect her from, because it was obvious she was just like Illiana. From the time she was an infant, she had fits of rage. She killed a bird when she was no more than two." A tear slid down his cheek. "That was on my wedding day to your mother. She soon progressed, though none of us realized it."

He appeared bewildered. "How does a child know about poisons? We never found out exactly how she murdered Julian. Of course, we didn't suspect her in the beginning. It was only when Katrine conceived you and we told her what we thought would be happy news that she became completely uncontrollable. She threatened to kill you, and she revealed to Katrine how she had murdered our son. Your mother fled, and it took me weeks to get all of the truth from Nikia."

"That's why you left me in America with Mother? To protect me, right?"

He nodded. "It was painful to be separated from you. I heard from your mother infrequently, and she sometimes sent pictures, but we both decided early on it was safer to give the appearance that I had ignored your existence." He squeezed her hand. "I've always loved you, *copia de meu inimiä*. I hope you believe that."

Anca nodded, feeling tears pressing at the back of her eyes. "What does that mean?" She tried to repeat the phrase, but the words sounded awkward on her tongue.

"Child of my heart." Valdemeer cleared his throat. "I love Nikia too — more than I hate her — and I am helpless about what to do with her. Perhaps if I hadn't locked Illiana away, she would have survived. Maybe Nikia would have been a softer person if she'd had a mother's love."

"Or maybe she would have been even more unhinged," Anca said softly.

"Maybe." He lifted his glass to drain it. When he set it down, his expression had lost its hint of sadness. His smile looked forced. "Enough of this talk. Whose move was it?"

"Yours," she said with a smile. A trace of fear lingered, but she pushed it aside with determination. Nikia was locked away, and she was safe as long as she remained so. If she decided to stay, she could deal with her half-sister. The thought of not returning to New York didn't bring the same surge of panic as it had earlier. She settled into the game with her father, feeling content and comfortable.

* * * * *

Nikia tossed aside the sliver of mirror with a screech of anger. She felt a measure of satisfaction when it crashed against the wall and shattered, though she knew she had lost a powerful tool with her childish act. "The bitch!" She turned on Sian, spitting out, "How dare she sit there so complacently, chatting with dear Father?" She kicked over the table near her and was pleased when the ceramic pitcher disintegrated on the floor.

"M'lady…"

"Hold your tongue." She slapped Sian, but it wasn't enough to relieve her rage. "Fetch me the girl."

A frown marred Sian's face. "The wench ordered to serve that bitch? Why do you want *her*?"

"Because I don't want you," she screamed. "Bring Helena to me now, or suffer my wrath."

With a sullen curtsey, Sian left the room, slamming the door behind her.

When she had gone, Nikia paced around the room, still seething over what her father had said about her. And how dare he speak that way about Illiana? She stamped her foot. He wouldn't have been so brave if he had known she observed him with the sliver of Seeing Mirror Illiana's mother had passed down to her.

Her body shook with anger, and her vision blurred. She wanted to kill someone, and she didn't care whom right then. Her preference was for her simpering half-sister and Valdemeer, but she knew anyone would do.

She must be careful not to injure Helena too much, she decided. It wouldn't do to kill the girl. Not only would she be depriving herself of future fun, but she would also incur Valdemeer's anger.

Since they had discovered her plot to kill Anca, Nikia knew she had to tread carefully, for a time. She mustn't be the focus of their attention until the blood-moon arrived. By then, they would be consumed with the ceremony and not be worrying about her. They wouldn't see it coming, she thought with a satisfied smile.

She lifted her head as the door squeaked and Sian reentered, dragging a reluctant Helena with her. The girl wore only a simple cotton shift, and she had obviously been preparing for bed. She wanted to oblige her, by all means. "Strip her and tie her to the bed, Sian."

"Please, mistress," the girl begged. Huge tears streaked down her cheeks. "Don't hurt me…"

Sian slapped her, seeming to take more pleasure than usual in the sound of her palm against flesh. "Speak only when given permission. You will soon learn."

As Sian saw to her task, Nikia went to her closet and fetched a small trunk. She opened it and examined her collection of toys. She had envisioned her initial seduction of Helena several times, but tonight all thoughts of being gentle had fled her mind. She wanted to strike out at someone, and the girl would do nicely.

She bypassed many of the toys that would bring pleasure and scooped up her prized possession—a supple leather whip with fringes at the end. Each fringe contained a tiny metal spike. It left a beautiful pattern of pain on anyone it struck.

Nikia briefly touched a large leather dildo, imagining the expression of agony Helena would wear when the monster ripped through her barrier of innocence. She licked her lips, anticipating a night of fun. Already, her black mood was lifting.

Helena's cry of pain at the first lash of the whip further buoyed her mood. As the whip ripped through the tender skin of the girl's thigh, she pictured her sister in front of her, bound and at her mercy. Her pussy spasmed with arousal, and she set Sian to work between her thighs as she poured her anger into Helena, using the whip to transfer it. Each cry was music to her ears, and she concentrated on savoring the experience.

# Chapter Twelve

Despite her best efforts to resist, Anca found herself drawn into the life of Corsovans. The more Demi showed her, the more she felt like she had come home. He seemed determined to show her everything during the week she had promised to stay, and she wasn't disappointed with what she observed.

The day they went to the port of Vachow, the dockworkers greeted her with a round of cheers. She toured shipyards, warehouses, and nearby homes before a small military vessel ferried her around the port. Afterward, the boat ventured out for a short cruise on the Black Sea, and they received an honor guard of several anglers' boats, sailing in a two-line formation behind them.

The village of Rij was small, but the people threw her an impromptu, grand celebration and spoke fondly of Katrine. Anca couldn't remember enjoying a day so much. It was heady to have people bowing and curtseying to her, while vying to grant her every wish.

Bulgainia, the capitol city, was larger than she expected, with a contemporary air, juxtaposed with ancient architecture, soaring turrets, and rounded roofs. The predominant building material was gray stone. Though everyone seemed to have some place to be or something to do, each person they met stopped and took time to welcome her home.

Grasov turned out to be a small farming community, harvesting wheat from verdant fields and fruit from huge orchards. The villagers' ways were simple and rustic, but they were warm and gracious.

Demi insisted she visit Sladavia, where he had been born. His parents had died years ago, but the community still greeted him like the prodigal son. The residents logged the timber conservatively, created crafts indigenous to Corsova, and took a few adventurous tourists on guided hunting tours through the surrounding forests. The people were busy, but they managed to put together a feast in her honor.

Anca couldn't help but wonder how much of the "impromptu" events were subtly arranged by Demi ahead of time, but she didn't mind his subterfuge. He was determined to show her the beauty of Corsova, and thus far, he had succeeded.

Since receiving a warm welcome at each place Demi took her, the cool reception of the residents of Necheau surprised her. It soon became obvious why Demi hadn't planned to take her to tour this village.

It was high in the mountains, and there was a chill in the air, despite the season. Anca huddled in a light jacket as they completed the last half-hour of the journey on foot, since the SUV couldn't climb any higher, and they had no horses.

At first glance, the village was as picturesque as the others she had seen. Children played in the streets, men with their sleeves rolled high gathered around a half-constructed building in the town square, and several women pitched in too. It was like stepping back to the 19th century.

Gradually, as they walked down the main street, the activity stopped. There was a quiet watchfulness about the adults, and the children seemed to sense the tension, because they scurried inside, with several leaving toys where they lay.

"Is something wrong?" she whispered to Demi.

He shrugged. "Our kind isn't welcome here. Most of the residents of Necheau are werewolves. Very territorial and not really friendly to members outside their pack."

If the silence had been unnerving before, it suddenly seemed deafening as a tall, broad-shouldered man stepped out of a two-story wooden house at the end of the main street. He had long, flowing black hair, scowling blue eyes, and an intimidating air preceded him as he stalked forward. He didn't offer a greeting or glance in her direction. "What brings you here, Nicodemus?" He virtually growled the words.

"Her Highness wanted to see the entire country."

He made a sound low in his throat, and it didn't sound polite. "Now she's seen it. Be on your way."

"Rica, she only wants to see—"

The man's menacing glower fastened briefly on Anca. "This is our territory, laid out by a treaty with your grandfather. We say who's allowed and who isn't." He glanced at the sun and squinted. "It's late in the morning. You'd best be on your way." Without another word, he turned his back on them and walked away. Conspicuously, the other residents followed his example.

Anca hugged herself and followed Demi down the mountain. When they were away from the village, she asked, "Why was he so unfriendly?"

"Rica was born unfriendly," he said with a hint of amusement, but he wasn't smiling. "As I said, the pack is territorial. They've spent centuries outrunning civilization.

Coming to Corsova was a last ditch solution for them when they arrived almost four hundred years ago. Your grandfather made them welcomed, and he even drew up a treaty to guarantee them land rights."

"Why would we need a treaty with them?" She didn't miss her own reference to the country being hers. She groaned under her breath at the slip.

"Werewolves are aggressive, and if they felt squeezed out, they might attack. Your grandfather used that as a pretext, but I think he just wanted to ensure they felt secure here." Demi sighed. "He had to demand something in return to legitimize the exchange."

She swallowed, wondering if the pack had good reason to mistrust their kind. "What did he ask for?" Visions of virgin sacrifices swept through her mind.

"Their blood, to enable our people to transform like they did. After a short time, it happened that a few of the wolves wanted our blood in return, to prolong their lives. We've sort of become a hybrid race, except for the stubborn ones like Rica." He shook his head, appearing perplexed. "He refuses to allow his people to take our blood. They have to sneak away to do so, and they generally aren't welcomed back after they've formed a blood-bond with a vampire."

"Is Starr…?"

"No. She was born a vampire, though she has formed a blood-bond with Lucian and Sorin. They're both outcasts in their village, since they chose our life. The three are inseparable."

"Does our kind ever marry theirs?"

He frowned. "Davinia, Ylenia's niece, married Rica's brother, but I've heard she isn't accepted among the people. It's difficult for her, and I'm surprised Rica allowed her to join their pack. Usually, if a wolf marries our kind—which is rare—they're forced to give up their place in the pack and live our way."

She sniffed with disapproval. "I hope he sees how narrow-minded he's being."

Demi laughed, but didn't bother to reply. His laugh held a note of skepticism, as if he doubted Rica could learn anything he didn't want to.

* * * * *

Almost unnoticed, the seven days Anca had agreed to stay slipped into ten, and then twelve. She didn't say anything about leaving, but she knew when Demi invited her for a run that he would push her for her answer. Was she staying and taking the Blood Oath, or was she returning to her real life that seemed less real all the time?

She didn't know yet.

They slipped into wolf-form before leaving the castle, and she matched his fast pace, taking advantage of the time to clear her mind and focus on her decision.

What he'd shown her of Corsova tempted her. She cared for the people in the country already, responding to their embrace of her presence. Each time she had ventured outside the castle, it was like reuniting with old friends she had never met.

And how could she leave her father when he was about to die? He was a proud man, but he was sensitive too. Anca found his hint of vulnerability endearing, and she could sense his need to make up for what he saw as abandoning her for years, even if it had been to protect her. She loved him fiercely and wanted to be with him until the end.

On the other hand, there was her mother. She had spoken to her by phone a couple of times, and each time Katrine insisted her life was in New York now, and she didn't want to return to Corsova. Her mother urged her to make her own decision, or as she phrased it, "the right decision," but Anca didn't know how she would cope alone. Katrine was healing well, but needed someone to look after her.

Also weighing heavily was her obligation to honor her birthright. It was her duty to take the Blood Oath, but she would sacrifice so much in doing so. It frightened her to know she or Demi could die, but Anca knew her father couldn't rule forever. She yearned for more time to decide, but the blood-moon was in two days.

She didn't have the luxury of waiting forty-six years for the next blood-moon, because of her father's age. He didn't look much older than his early sixties, but apparently, it was a characteristic of their kind to be visibly ageless as one grew older. The body still aged though, and death was inevitable for even the Protector of Corsova.

Most of all, there was Demi to think about. He had sworn to follow her back to New York if that was her choice, but he clearly belonged in Corsova. She already felt the connection to the land he and Ylenia had spoken of, and she couldn't bear the thought of tearing him away from the only way of life he had ever known.

Nor could she contemplate separating from him. She loved him.

Demi stopped running, interrupting her thoughts. He hadn't spoken to her during their journey, probably realizing she was thinking. He dropped something from his mouth and turned to her before transforming back to his true form. "Our spot," he said with a wink.

It was, Anca realized. This was the place they had stopped during their last run, made love, and slept through most of the night. With a start, she realized it was also the place from her vision on the train. She looked up.

*The night sky was a black canvas, with thousands of stars twinkling overhead. She had never seen anything like it in New York. She could hear the wind blowing softly through the trees. The lone cry of a wolf rose with haunting intensity, before others soon joined in, and their cries echoed down the mountainside. The pack was close, but she felt no fear.*

*Without thought, she shed her wolf-form and curled up beside Demi on a bed of rose bay. She tilted her head as his lips caressed her neck, tickling when he breathed against her skin. "Umm, that feels good."*

*He cupped her breast, gently thumbing her nipple. "So does that."*

*She laughed softly and touched his cheek as she shifted in his arms.*

*He took hold of her hand and brought it to his mouth. His tongue traced her palm and moved down.*

Anca threw back her head as sensations coursed through her. She gazed upward, noting the tumescent moon was nearly full, and it had a strange pinkish cast. She looked away, but it drew her gaze again. Each time her eyes sought it, her heartbeat accelerated. She turned her head at the touch of lips against her wrist.

"Soon, it will be time," Demi said, and his lips tickled her skin. "In two nights, the moon will be blood-red."

"Yes." She started to share her doubts, but her eyes widened when Demi's teeth penetrated the skin at her wrist, finding the vein unerringly. He had never fed from her before. "Demi?" she asked in a hoarse voice as he sucked gently.

She gasped as the initial pain faded to an intense pleasure. Anca held her breath, and her eyes closed of their own volition. As his tongue slid over the wound, probing gently, she opened her eyes to slits and watched the play of emotions on Demi's face. She could see his arousal, but more obvious was his tenderness.

As his throat worked convulsively, swallowing her blood, she unfurled and lay back on the soft bed of rose bay, closing her eyes again, absorbing the pleasure from this new form of intimacy. During the past twelve days, they had tried many things, but not this. She wondered why he had waited.

He retracted his fangs and released her wrist. "You weren't ready," he said, answering her unspoken question. "Part of you still doubted what you were, what we are."

He moved up her body. Her blood smeared his lips, and Anca lifted her head to hasten the meeting of their mouths. Rather than kiss him, she traced her tongue across his lips, licking away the traces of her blood. The flavor was pungent and coppery, but with an underlying sweetness that made her yearn for more. She punctured his lower lip with her canine and licked the tiny wound as he hissed with a combination of pleasure and pain.

Demi had been sprawled beside her, but now he broke away and rolled over to straddle her. He braced his hands on the ground, bracketing her head, and leaned forward to kiss her. His cock pressed into the softness of her stomach, and her pussy flooded with desire.

Anca tilted her head, offering her neck for his possession, but he ignored the temptation. "We rarely take blood from the neck, *dragostia*. It's too dangerous, even for our kind. You might not heal fast enough to prevent losing too much blood."

His lips parted hers gently, and his tongue ventured inside to explore her moist depths. She groaned low in her throat as his tongue slid across hers. She tried to still his movements, but his tongue darted from hers to trace her teeth.

His tongue retreated, and he eased his weight down on her more fully. As Demi's face burrowed into the bend of her neck, one of his hands squeezed her breast. He rubbed a nipple between his fingers, causing the sensitive nub to harden at his expert touch.

His other hand traveled down her side, exploring her ribs, pausing to span her waist, pat her hip, and then slide along her thigh.

Anca stiffened as he sought out her pussy. He was going too slowly. She longed to feel his cock inside her pussy, and anticipation had her gyrating her hips impatiently.

He chuckled again as he stroked her swollen pussy lips, wet with her own dew, but he didn't venture between them.

She grunted and arched her hips, demanding without words that he fulfill his unspoken promise.

Demi's breath was hot against her neck when he said, "So impatient."

She tangled her hands in his hair, urging his mouth closer to her neck as she arched her hips. "Please," she whispered. "I trust you."

He hesitated.

"I want to," she assured him. She found the thought of him drinking from her intoxicating and arousing. The threat of danger only added to her excitement.

"I live to serve you," he said with a trace of gentle mockery. Seconds later, his fangs penetrated the vein at her neck at the same time his fingers slid inside her pussy and sought out her twitching clit. He found her wet and ready, and she gave voice to her passion as he fingered her with slow thrusts.

"More," she urged, not sure if she wanted him to drink more deeply or thrust faster.

He broke away from her neck, carefully lapping up the rivulets of blood. Seconds later, he lifted his head to meet her eyes. "You're healing."

She nodded, feeling the wound closing as he spoke. "Take me, Demi." Anca heard him rustling the flowers and lifted her head to see what he was doing. She watched as he ran his hand through the rose bay. "What are you doing?"

"I spat out a condom here," he said. "I didn't have anywhere else to carry it, and by the time we got here, I couldn't wait to get rid of it. I didn't think to notice where it dropped." He made a low sound of triumph and held up the package. "Ah ha."

She grinned at him and lay back with her thighs spread wide. It didn't take him long to come to her, and she gasped when he joined their bodies with one hard thrust. As Demi eased himself down on top of her, Anca grasped his shoulders and arched her hips upward, taking in all of him.

She set the pace, moving fast and urgent, aching for completion. Anca took his hand and guided it to her pussy, and he immediately began to rub her clit. She closed her eyes and circled her hips slowly while thrusting against him. Soon, her pace increased again, and he matched it with the thrust of his cock and the quickness of his fingers.

Anca pressed her face against his chest as her orgasm neared. It was the most natural thing in the world to sink her fangs into the vein above his heart. As rich blood pumped into her mouth, she felt his cock spasm and pump hot fluid inside the condom. The blood trickled from her mouth, and she swallowed as fast as she could, even as her pussy contracted with an orgasm.

She crushed him against her, surprised by her own strength, as she removed her mouth from his wound. Her pussy continued spasming, and aftermath caused her limbs to quiver. As her heartbeat slowed, Anca noticed his did too, as her ear was near his heart. She took a deep breath, feeling exhaustion catch up with her. She stretched, and he rolled away, but still held her close to his side.

Anca turned onto her side to examine the wound she had made. It was already scabbing over, so she hadn't done too much damage. "Did it hurt?"

He shrugged. "A little, but it also felt good."

"Yes," she said in a whisper. She trailed her fingers through his light dusting of chest hair. "I've decided."

He stiffened, and a hint of wariness crept into his expression. "About the Blood Oath?"

She nodded. "I'll do it."

He sagged with relief, but he still asked, "Are you sure that's what you want? There's no going back."

She gave him a shaky smile. "I know. I'm afraid, but I know you'll be with me. That's the most important thing to me." She steeled herself, gathering her courage. "I love you, Demi."

He exhaled harshly, and then pulled her tightly against him. "You don't know how long I've waited to hear you say that."

She nodded, unable to speak with her face pressed against his chest. When he loosened his grip, she tilted her neck to look up at him. "I wanted to say it days ago, but it didn't feel right until I'd decided. I didn't want to tell you I loved you and then leave. Now that I've decided, I can shout it if I want to."

He gave her a crooked grin. "Go ahead. No one will hear, except maybe a few wolves."

She felt a little embarrassed, but she raised her voice into a shout. "I, Anca Draganescu, love Nicodemus Golina."

A plethora of howls responded to her shouted announcement. Each seemed to hold a note of approval and perhaps a little amusement. Anca grinned at him before curving herself against him and laying her head on his chest. She was at peace with her decision and content in his arms.

# Chapter Thirteen

The night of the blood-moon arrived, and Anca was more nervous than she had ever been. Helena came to assist her with the proper garb for the ceremony. She noticed the girl moved slowly and winced each time she lifted her arms. She frowned with concern as the girl winced yet again when she stood up from straightening the ankle-length hem. "Helena, are you okay?"

The girl gave her a shaky smile and smoothed a wrinkle from Anca's white velvet robe. It was so pure a white that standing next to it gave her already-washed-out complexion an even more ghostly element. "Fine, m'lady."

Anca continued to watch her as she laced the bodice of the robe and tied it in a neat bow. As Helena stepped back, the sleeve of her gray robe slid up, revealing long slashes. Though scabbed, they still looked terrible. She took the girl's hand before she could draw away and pushed back the sleeve. She inhaled sharply. "My God. Who did this?"

Helena tried to tug away, and she refused to meet her eyes. "Really, it's nothing, mistress — "

Anca stepped off the small stool she had stood on. She dropped Helena's right arm before taking her left and pushing up the sleeve. The same wounds marred her skin. "What did this?"

Helena shook her head as her eyes darted frantically around the room.

She made her voice firm. "Tell me now."

"But—"

"I demand you tell me."

Tears poured down the younger girl's face. "I-it was a wh-whip, Your Highness." Sobs shook her frail shoulders, but she winced and pulled away when Anca patted her back.

"Take off your robe." When she saw the instinctive way Helena covered her breasts and drew away, she hastened to reassure her. "I'm not going to hurt you, but I need to see how badly you're injured."

With the air of a martyr, Helena unlaced her dress as she turned around. She let the dress fall to her waist, careful to preserve her modesty.

What she saw nauseated her. Scores of whip marks crisscrossed each other. They had healed over, but Anca thought a couple of the deeper ones were infected. Tenderly, she drew the robe up her back and over the marks, holding it in place while Helena's shaking fingers refastened her laces.

Anca turned her carefully, but she couldn't hide the anger in her trembling voice. "Who did this to you?"

Helena's hair hid her face and muffled her voice, but the name was still audible. "Nikia."

Rage coursed through Anca, and without thought, she forced herself into her half-sister's thoughts. She cried out in pain as Nikia threw her out with a violent wrench and placed a block between them. She swayed unsteadily and grasped the bedpost.

"M'lady? Are you ill?" Concern reflected from Helena's eyes.

She shook her head and drew in a deep breath. "No. I'm not sure what happened. I think I tried to get into her thoughts, and she forced me out."

When she had regained control, Anca took Helena's hand and led her to the bed. She eased her down gently and reached for the box of tissues on the nightstand. "You have to tell me what happened." She expected resistance, but there was a trace of relief in Helena's eyes as the story poured from her.

What she heard served to stoke her anger with Nikia, but also had her crying quietly along with the younger girl cradled in her arms. When Helena's words and tears were spent, she rocked her. "I promise you she'll never touch you again. Once the ceremony is over, I'll deal with Nikia."

She sounded like a timid mouse. "How, Your Highness?"

Anca hesitated. The answer was obvious, but did she have the ability to impose a death sentence on someone? She had learned during her stay in Corsova that the American legal system was a foreign concept here. The people lived by the rule of the Protectorate, so they'd better hope it was fair. She bit her lip. "I'll send her away."

Helena's shoulders sagged, and she pulled away. "Lord Nicodemus will be here soon to collect you." She gestured to the tray she had arrived with earlier in the evening. "Ylenia said you would both need to drink this potion."

As if her words had summoned him, there was a knock at the door. Helena rushed forward to answer it, and she curtsied to Demi as he stepped inside.

He temporarily distracted her from the problem with Nikia. Anca couldn't resist a small sigh of pleasure as she examined Demi in the sapphire-blue robe. She wasn't accustomed to seeing men in anything but trousers and shorts, but he didn't look at all feminine in the flowing robe. The cut emphasized the breadth of his shoulders and the narrowness of his waist. The color brought dark-blue flecks to his black eyes and caused his hair to shine more brilliantly in the light.

He approached her, pulling her from the bed and into his arms for a quick, hard kiss. "I've missed you."

She bit back a giggle. "You saw me this morning, before you left my chambers."

He grinned down at her, but the edges of his mouth trembled almost imperceptibly. He seemed nervous. "That's too long."

Anca didn't mention her own case of nerves as Helena approached with two pewter goblets of the potion Ylenia sent with her. She took one and gave the girl an encouraging smile. She thought about reassuring her again that Nikia wouldn't hurt her anymore, but she didn't think Helena would want Demi to know. She would tell him, but not when the girl was in hearing distance.

Demi eyed the potion with a frown. "What's this?"

Helena's eyes remained downcast. "I know not, m'lord. Ylenia told me to have you both drink a cup."

He sniffed it, grimacing slightly. With a jovial smile, he clinked his goblet against Anca's. "Cheers."

"Bottoms up," she said with an equally fake smile and brought the cup to her lips. It smelled foul, but tasted faintly like apricots and honey. "Not bad." She finished the rest of it in one long drink, as Demi did the same.

He returned the cups to Helena and held out his hand.

Anca folded hers in his and took a step to join him by his side. The room started spinning, and bile rushed up the back of her throat. Her stomach heaved, and her eyes seemed weighted. She opened her mouth to alert Demi that something was wrong.

He interrupted her by uttering a single word. "Poison." He fell heavily on the stone floor.

Anca reached for him, but her arm felt disconnected from her body. The room whirled faster, but her eyes managed to settle briefly on the serving girl.

Tears swam in Helena's widened eyes. Her fingers were in her mouth, and she appeared to be biting down hard to keep from crying out. She pulled them away and shook her head. "It's not poison, m'lady. Only a sleeping dram."

"Why?" she managed to ask, as she fell beside Demi.

Helena knelt beside her, smoothing the hair off her brow. "I'm sorry, m'lady. I had no choice. I'm afraid of her."

"It's okay," she whispered, knowing her half-sister was behind this. Nikia's name echoed through Anca's mind as she passed out.

\* \* \* \* \*

She awoke lying on the bed. Anca struggled to move and found her arms bound to the bedposts. A pressure on her chest made her lift her head and look down. She frowned at the contraption. She could feel it clamped around her waist, and she was lying on it. It seemed to serve no purpose except to hold the wickedly sharp stake aimed inches from her heart.

She opened her mouth to scream for help and realized she was gagged. She heard movement beside her and turned her head to see Demi bound with his arms at his sides, clamped in by a device identical to hers, with the spike resting against his heart. She made a quizzical sound, and he turned his head.

His eyes reflected his fear, and he said something, but the gag muffled his words beyond comprehension. He closed his eyes. *Nikia's treachery.*

*Yes. What do we do?*

*We have to escape.* He grunted.

*How?*

They froze as a cold laugh sounded from the right, out of their range of sight. Nikia stepped into view, leaning over Anca. "You can't, sister. You're tied securely, and if you had plans of transforming," she caressed the spike near Anca's heart, "think again. Silver poisons werewolves, and you have enough of their characteristics to get deathly ill from it—assuming you survived the spike penetrating your heart."

*Why?* Anca cried out, using her full mental powers in case Nikia had a block in place again.

"Because I'm taking the Blood Oath. It's my right, not yours." Anger sparkled in Nikia's eyes. "You can't usurp me of my rightful place."

*You'll die—*

"Lies!" Nikia waved her hand. "Ylenia wants to keep me from my heritage, that's all. I'm not good enough for them because of who my mother was." She leaned closer, until her face was inches from Anca's. "She wasn't saintly like the bitch who produced you, so they want to eradicate her bloodline, but I won't let them."

Anca searched for a way to reason with Nikia, but soon realized there wasn't any reasoning with the mad. The gleam of insanity shone in her eyes. They couldn't stop her with mere words.

"You can't stop me at all," Nikia hissed. "I'll soon have everything I need." She beckoned to Sian, who approached carrying the golden chalice and a sharp dagger. "I need your blood and the pendant." Her eyes turned to Demi. "His blood too, and our dear father's, and I'll be the rightful ruler."

Anca tried to steel herself for the prick of the dagger when Nikia pushed back the voluminous sleeve of her white robe and pressed the tip against the bend of her elbow. She cried out when it slid through her flesh, but the cloth in her mouth muffled the volume.

Nikia's eyes never strayed from the sight of Anca's blood flowing into the goblet. It was only when the wound stopped flowing that she handed the dagger and goblet to Sian. "Get his." She directed a scorching look in Demi's direction. "I have no wish to touch *him*."

As Sian moved around the bed to collect Demi's blood, Nikia's fingers moved to the laces at Anca's robe. "Now for the pendant, dear sister."

Anca tried to twist away, but she couldn't evade Nikia. Within seconds, her breasts were exposed, and Nikia had unfastened the pendant. She couldn't hold back a mournful moan when Nikia removed the pendant.

Her moan turned to a cry of shock when Nikia tweaked her nipple. She shook her head and redoubled her efforts to move away, but was securely restrained. The gag muffled her scream of outrage when Nikia bent her head and licked her breast. *Don't touch me!*

"Tasty," Nikia said before her fangs sank into the soft flesh of Anca's breast. She suckled for a couple of seconds before lifting her head. "If I had more time, dear sister..." She sighed. "Perhaps I'll keep you around as my plaything for a while, until I tire of you." She cupped Anca's other breast as she knelt and licked her cheek. "I'll teach you how to use your tongue." Her voice lowered to a sensual whisper. "I'll teach you to submit."

She stood up and glared at Demi. "I'm afraid I have no use for your lover though. When I've completed the ritual, he'll be the first to die." She waved her hand at Sian, and they hurried across the room. Nikia didn't pause to look back as she swept through the door, slamming it behind her.

Anca turned her head so she could see Demi. *We have to get out of here and stop her. She'll die if she takes the Blood Oath.*

*Who cares? I'm more worried about missing the moon phase. If you don't take the Oath now, there won't be another chance. I'm sure she's already gone after your father.* As he spoke, Demi twisted against the silver restraint, hissing when the spike raked his skin.

*How do we get out of these?*

*There's only one way I can think of.* His gaze locked with hers. *I love you, Anca. All that matters is for you to stop Nikia and complete the ceremony.*

She guessed what he planned to do even as he did it. She cried out in protest as he transformed into wolf-form.

Demi spat out the gag as he howled with agony. The spike had penetrated his chest, and it seemed to take all his strength to pull away from it. His breath came in shallow pants as he turned back to his human form. "Ah, it hurts, *dragostia*." His forced smile seemed weak as he lurched across the bed and untied her restraints with shaking hands. He opened the restraint with a click

As soon as she was free, Anca sat up and rolled toward him, touching his pale face. "Are you dying?"

"Don't know," he said amid pants.

She hugged him against her. "Tell me what to do to save you."

"Blood. Need blood."

She didn't hesitate to push open the unlaced bodice of her robe and offer her neck. She groaned with pain as Demi's fangs sank through her skin. He didn't have the same finesse as last time, and she wasn't aroused, so it hurt enough to bring tears to her eyes. She endured stoically as he drank for several minutes.

She became light-headed and started to pull away just as he broke contact. Some color had reappeared in his cheeks, but he still looked terrible. "Will you live?"

He nodded. "It's going to take a long time to heal though. I won't be much use to you tonight."

She rolled out of bed, helping him. Anca tried to brace him against her, but he pulled away and stood tall. "Now what?"

"We have to find Valdemeer. She needs his blood to complete the ceremony. If she hasn't gotten to him yet, it isn't too late to stop her."

Demi surprised her by matching her frantic pace— though not without difficulty—as they rushed to Valdemeer's chambers. He walked with an unsteady gait and swayed from time to time, but he didn't falter. He seemed to be running solely on adrenaline or determination, but there was no time to allow him to rest.

Valdemeer's partially opened door and the lack of a guard in the hallway caused Anca's stomach to clench with fear. She pushed open the oak door and rushed into his room. She cried out when she saw him sprawled on the stone floor. A large puddle of blood surrounded him.

"Papa," she cried as she ran to him. She was marginally aware of Demi catching up with her and crouching beside her as she knelt to check on Valdemeer. She felt his ravaged throat and cried out at the thread of a pulse she found. She cried out again as his eyes snapped open, and he gripped her wrist with surprising strength. "You're alive."

"Dying," he said in a slow whisper. "Take my blood."

She shook her head. "You'll die if we take more."

His eyes moved to Demi, and he nodded.

Anca looked up in time to see Demi nod and stand up. When he made his way to the mini-bar to get a glass, she shook her head, mouthing the word, "No." She looked down at her father. "We can't do this. I don't want you to die."

His mouth was slack, and his eyes had started to glaze. He seemed to find thinking easier than speaking. *Always meant to die, Anca...part of the ritual.*

She shook her head, not understanding—or refusing to believe.

*Yes,* he insisted. *The way of things. Passing of old to new...my power to you. Can't change it.*

She glared at him. "You should have told me. I wouldn't have agreed to do it if you'd told me."

*I know. Couldn't tell you...made Demi swear not to.* He found the strength to squeeze her hand gently. *This is our way.*

Demi returned to them, holding the snifter. "I have a container, m'lord."

"Do it," he said shakily.

Anca couldn't watch as Demi pressed on the wound at her father's neck to cause more blood to flow. She pressed her hands over her eyes and began to sob.

*Love you, copia de meu inimiä. Take care of Demi, and guard our ways.*

"It's not fair," she whispered. Anca grasped his hand between hers as tears flowed down her cheeks. "I love you, Papa. I don't want to lose you now."

*Hurry, copia. You must stop her. Don't want Nikia to die, and you...take Oath before moon moves...alignment.* With a feeble reciprocal squeeze, Valdemeer's eyes closed. His grip became slack, and his last breath passed his lips.

Anca couldn't seem to pry loose her hold as Demi urged her up. She wanted to stay beside her father and mourn his passing, but there was no time. "Goodbye, Papa," she said softly as she got to her feet.

Demi set a brisk pace, moving with more grace than he had exhibited earlier.

Anca swiped her cheeks. "Are you stronger?"

He nodded. "I'm still weak though." He grasped the railing of the stairway leading to the tower, leaning heavily against the wall. He handed her the glass of her father's blood. "Take this. I might drop it."

She held it reluctantly, refusing to look down at the last precious drops wrung from Valdemeer. She bit back another sob, knowing she had to control her emotions. If she broke down now, she wouldn't be in any shape to confront Nikia, and too much rested on stopping her half-sister's scheme.

They made poor time, hampered by Demi's inability to climb without dragging himself up each step by use of the banister. Halfway up, he waved her on ahead of him. "Go, Anca. I'll catch up, but you have to stop her." He pointed to the window at the top of the tower, craning his neck. "The moon will pass out of alignment soon."

With an uncertain glance at the snifter of blood in her hand, she said, "What about...?"

"I'll be there in time." He took the blood from her. "I won't drop it. I swear."

She nodded, seeing by the intensity in his eyes he would protect it at all costs. "I love you." Anca broke into a run, taking the stairs two at a time as they curved around the tower. When she reached the landing, there was only one door, and she plunged through it without thought.

She skidded to a halt, shocked by what she saw. A blood-red orb reflected the moonlight onto a dais where the chalice sat. Her pendant fitted in the slot at the base of the goblet, and it glowed as intensely as the orb aligned with the moonbeam as it absorbed the reflected light. Nikia's hand grasped the goblet, and she uttered something in Corsovan.

Anca's eyes moved to where Starr stood, holding an old parchment in bound hands. The young woman shook with fear, and her voice was unsteady. She also spoke Corsovan, but the words got lost amid the sobs issuing from her.

When Anca looked down, she saw why the girl was crying. Ylenia was lying facedown on the floor in a heap. A deep-red stain had soaked through the back of her silver robe, and she wasn't moving. Obviously, she had tried to stop Nikia or had failed to cooperate.

As Starr finished speaking and Nikia raised the goblet, Anca remembered her purpose, and she rushed forward. "No, don't do it. Papa told me to keep you from killing yourself." She ran, but the goblet touched Nikia's lips before she was even in reach. "Don't do it, Nikia. Please."

Nikia didn't pause. She gulped the contents of the chalice in greedy swallows. Some of the blood dripped from the rim and trickled down her chin, but she didn't pause to wipe it away. She didn't stop until she had consumed every drop.

She slammed the goblet onto the dais and rounded on Anca. Her brownish-green eyes held a red glint. "The power. I can't believe it. I can feel it flowing through every pore...my heart pumping, sending it throughout..." She broke off as a strange expression flitted across her face. She clutched her chest, seeming no longer enthralled by the power flooding her.

Her expression was quizzical as she met Anca's sad eyes. Nikia held out her hand, seeming to be pleading for something, but having no voice to utter her request. Her eyes widened, and she coughed. Blood poured from her mouth, staining her white robe. She fell to her knees, and a piercing scream freed itself from her throat.

She looked up, meeting Anca's gaze again. *It wasn't supposed to be like this*, Nikia said as she collapsed on the stone floor.

Anca heard footsteps behind her and saw Demi approaching slowly. She rushed to him, embracing him. "I tried to stop her, but she wouldn't listen."

One of his hands smoothed her hair. "She was beyond hearing. She craved power so badly she couldn't see reason."

Starr approached timidly. "You have to hurry. There're only a few minutes left."

Anca wrapped her arm around Demi's waist, and he leaned against her as they walked to the dais. She saw Starr fumbling with the chalice, trying to hold it in her bound hands. She leaned Demi against the dais, making sure he had a secure grasp, and turned to Starr. "Let me untie you."

Starr held out her hands, and Anca struggled with the rope, not making any headway with unraveling the complicated knots.

"She had a dagger." Starr jerked her head in Nikia's direction.

Anca went to Nikia, rolling her onto her back. Her eyes widened when she realized her sister breathed shallowly. "She's still alive." She touched her throat, finding a weak, but steady, pulse. She noticed Nikia's eyelids moving back and forth rapidly, and opened one of her lids. Her eyes were twitching in a semblance of REM sleep. "I think she's in a coma," she said uncertainly.

"There's no time to worry about her right now," Demi said. "Find the dagger, Anca."

She nodded and looked down. Nothing stuck out of Nikia's belt, and there wasn't anything in her pockets. "It isn't here—"

"Look out, Your Highness," Starr screamed.

Anca looked up in time to see the woman who had assisted Nikia by taking Demi's blood rushing toward her with a dagger held over her head. She had been in the shadows of the corner, apparently forgotten by Starr. She rolled out of the way, as the mad woman lunged at her. She kicked out with both of her feet, catching her attacker in the stomach.

With a breathless groan, she fell onto the floor, dropping the dagger in the process. Anca rolled forward and plucked it away before gaining her feet. She searched for some way to bind her, but the only rope she saw was on Starr's wrists.

"Hurry," Starr urged.

Reluctantly, Anca grasped the sturdy handle of the dagger and hit the woman against the temple, causing her to crumple into unconsciousness. Absurdly, she found herself saying, "Sorry," as she hurried back to the dais.

She freed Starr, and the other woman used her sleeve to wipe out the dregs of blood remaining in the goblet. Then she held out her hand for the snifter of blood from Valdemeer. It had started to congeal, and she grimaced as she dumped it in. "Quickly, I need your blood, Your Highnesses."

Anca passed the dagger to Demi, unable to cut herself. He exhaled sharply when he sliced his forearm and held it over the goblet. When he took her hand and exposed her wrist, she closed her eyes. The blade was sharp and penetrated easily. She opened her eyes again when he moved her wrist over the goblet. The wound closed seconds later, and the chalice brimmed with crimson liquid.

Starr rotated the goblet on the dais and positioned the pendant to absorb the beam from the orb. "Lord Nicodemus, you begin, since you know the Oath. English will be fine, for Her Highness's sake."

He put his hand on the base and began speaking. "I acknowledge and embrace my duty as companion to the Protector of Corsova. I pledge my life to protect hers, and I vow to honor the ways of our people."

"Take a drink," Starr directed.

Demi lifted the chalice and swallowed some of the blood before returning it to the dais. He aligned it perfectly before moving aside so Anca could stand by the dais. He put his arm around her, offering silent support.

She grasped the base of the chalice. "What do I do?"

"Repeat after me." Starr took the parchment from her pocket. "I acknowledge and embrace my duty as the Protector of our people."

Anca repeated the line, pausing uncertainly when her hand began to tingle. She finished the first section when Starr admonished her to hurry.

Starr continued reading when she finished speaking. "I will protect our people and traditions. I will remain loyal to our ways. I vow to be a just and fair leader. I accept my burden with grace. I am the Protector of the old ways, and shepherd of the people. I am Corsova."

Anca had to have Starr repeat part of the Oath, and again she was distracted when the tingling crept up her arm and spread throughout her body. By the time she uttered the last word, she was aware of the tingling in every part of her body.

"Now drink, mistress. Drink it all."

As Anca finished the goblet of cooling blood, grimacing at its congealed state, Starr spoke in Corsovan, finalizing the ritual. When she returned the chalice to the dais, her body burned with energy, though it was painless. She turned to share her wonder with Demi and was astounded to see he had healed completely and looked restored.

He touched his chest. "The power healed me. I'd forgotten that would happen." He held out his arms.

Anca went willingly, burying her face against the softness of his sapphire robe. Tears leaked from her eyes, and she didn't know the exact reason she cried. Grief for her father, an overwhelming sense of power, and fear of the unknown were all reasons for her sobs, but there was something indefinable too. Perhaps pity for her sister, she decided tentatively.

He held her until the storm passed, murmuring soothing words in Corsovan.

When Anca lifted her head, she felt marginally better. "What happens now, my love?"

"We live our lives and do our duty." He kissed her gently. "We follow our destiny."

Sadness shadowed her eyes. "My father…"

"He was ready, Anca. He knew what would happen, and his last days were happier for having met you."

She nodded, and her gaze settled on Ylenia before moving to Nikia and the woman on the floor near her. "So much suffering and death. What will we do with Nikia?"

"We'll send her away to be cared for. There are no facilities in Corsova to meet her needs, and none secure enough to hold her if she awakens. She can't be allowed back into our country." Demi's face tightened when his gaze settled on Sian. "She will also be banished. Death is no more than she deserves, but…"

She nodded, understanding his reservations without having him utter them. Doubt seized her as she wondered how she would ever live up to the Oath she had taken.

Anca looked up, meeting Demi's eyes, and found her answer. His love and support would see her through.

# Author's Note:

When I set out to create a country to act as a haven for those who weren't fully human, I wanted it to be realistic. My first step was to find a suitable location for a "vampire" world. When I thought of vampires, Romania came to mind, but I didn't want to be obvious. Eastern Europe still seemed like the perfect setting for such a country, and I scoured maps. Eventually, I "borrowed" a section of the Ukraine and made it into Corsova.

There was more to creating a country than deciding on a name. I had to figure out geography, economy, flora, fauna, and culture. In order to have Corsova mesh with the other countries in the region, I did a lot of research on Moldova, Romania, and the Ukraine. Taking the best parts of each country, I formed a composite that became Corsova.

Corsovan is spoken a few times throughout the book, and the language is based heavily on Romanian, which had the easiest translator to find online and understand. The addition of a few letters transformed Romanian into Corsovan.

Any inaccuracies in the real places mentioned are a byproduct of artistic license.

## About the author:

Kit Tunstall lives in Idaho with her husband and dog-son. She started reading at the age of three and hasn't stopped since. Love of the written word, and a smart marriage to a supportive man, led her to a full-time career in writing. Romances have always intrigued her, and erotic romance is a natural extension because it more completely explores the emotions between the hero and heroine. That, and it sure is fun to write.

Kit welcomes mail from readers. You can write to her c/o Ellora's Cave Publishing at 1056 Home Ave. Akron, Oh. 44310-3502.

# Why an electronic book?

We live in the Information Age—an exciting time in the history of human civilization in which technology rules supreme and continues to progress in leaps and bounds every minute of every hour of every day. For a multitude of reasons, more and more avid literary fans are opting to purchase e-books instead of paperbacks. The question to those not yet initiated to the world of electronic reading is simply: *why?*

1. *Price.* An electronic title at Ellora's Cave Publishing and Cerridwen Press runs anywhere from 40-75% less than the cover price of the <u>exact same title</u> in paperback format. Why? Cold mathematics. It is less expensive to publish an e-book than it is to publish a paperback, so the savings are passed along to the consumer.

2. *Space.* Running out of room to house your paperback books? That is one worry you will never have with electronic novels. For a low one-time cost, you can purchase a handheld computer designed specifically for e-reading purposes. Many e-readers are larger than the average handheld, giving you plenty of screen room. Better yet, hundreds of titles can be stored within your new library—a single microchip. (Please note that Ellora's Cave and Cerridwen Press does not endorse any specific brands. You can check our website at www.ellorascave.com or

www.cerridwenpress.com for customer recommendations we make available to new consumers.)

3. *Mobility*. Because your new library now consists of only a microchip, your entire cache of books can be taken with you wherever you go.

4. *Personal preferences are accounted for*. Are the words you are currently reading too small? Too large? Too...**ANNOYING**? Paperback books cannot be modified according to personal preferences, but e-books can.

5. *Instant gratification*. Is it the middle of the night and all the bookstores are closed? Are you tired of waiting days—sometimes weeks—for online and offline bookstores to ship the novels you bought? Ellora's Cave Publishing sells instantaneous downloads 24 hours a day, 7 days a week, 365 days a year. Our e-book delivery system is 100% automated, meaning your order is filled as soon as you pay for it.

Those are a few of the top reasons why electronic novels are displacing paperbacks for many an avid reader. As always, Ellora's Cave and Cerridwen Press welcomes your questions and comments. We invite you to email us at service@ellorascave.com, service@cerridwenpress.com or write to us directly at: 1056 Home Ave. Akron OH 44310-3502.

# COMING TO A BOOKSTORE NEAR YOU!

# ELLORA'S CAVE
# 2005
## BEST SELLING AUTHORS TOUR

# THE
# ELLORA'S CAVE
## LIBRARY

Stay up to date with Ellora's Cave Titles
in Print with our Quarterly Catalog.

To recieve a catalog,
send an email with your name
and mailing address to:

## CATALOG@ELLORASCAVE.COM

or send a letter or postcard
with your mailing address to:
Catalog Request
c/o Ellora's Cave Publishing, Inc.
1337 Commerce Drive #13
Stow, OH 44224

NEED A MORE EXCITING
WAY TO PLAN YOUR DAY?

# ELLORA'S
## CAVEMEN
2006 CALENDAR

COMING THIS FALL

Discover for yourself why readers can't get enough of the multiple award-winning publisher Ellora's Cave. Whether you prefer e-books or paperbacks, be sure to visit EC on the web at www.ellorascave.com for an erotic reading experience that will leave you breathless.

www.ellorascave.com

Printed in the United States
38940LVS00004B/373-396